ARTEMIS FOWL

THE OPAL DECEPTION

THE GRAPHIC NOVEL

Adapted by

EOIN COLFER
&
ANDREW DONKIN

Art by GIOVANNI RIGANO

Color by PAOLO

Color Separation by S

Lettering by CHI

D1292501

DISNEP • HYPERION BOOKS

Los Angeles   New York

Adapted from the novel *Artemis Fowl: The Opal Deception*
Text copyright © 2014 by Eoin Colfer
Illustrations copyright © 2014 by Giovanni Rigano

Printed in the United States of America
First Edition
10 9 8 7 6 5 4 3 2 1
V381-8386-5-14105

Library of Congress Cataloging-in-Publication Data
Colfer, Eoin.
Artemis Fowl. The opal deception : the graphic novel / adapted by Eoin Colfer and Andrew Donkin ; art by Giovanni Rigano ; color by Paolo Lamanna ; lettering by Chris Dickey. —First edition.
    pages cm — (Artemis Fowl ; 4)
"Adapted from the novel Artemis Fowl: The Opal Deception."
Summary: After his last run-in with the fairies, Artemis Fowl's mind was wiped of memories of the world belowground and any goodness grudgingly learned is now gone with the young genius reverting to his criminal lifestyle.
ISBN 978-1-4231-4528-8 (hardcover) — ISBN 978-1-4231-4549-3 (paperback)
1. Graphic novels. [1. Graphic novels. 2. Adventure and adventurers—Fiction. 3. Pixies—Fiction. 4. Fairies—Fiction. 5. Magic—Fiction. 6. Computers—Fiction. 7. England—Fiction.]
I. Donkin, Andrew. II. Rigano, Giovanni, illustrator. III. Title. IV. Title: Opal deception.
PZ7.7.C645Aso 2014
741.5'9415—dc23   2014004121

Visit www.DisneyBooks.com and www.artemisfowl.com

HAPTER 1:

TOTALLY OBSESSED

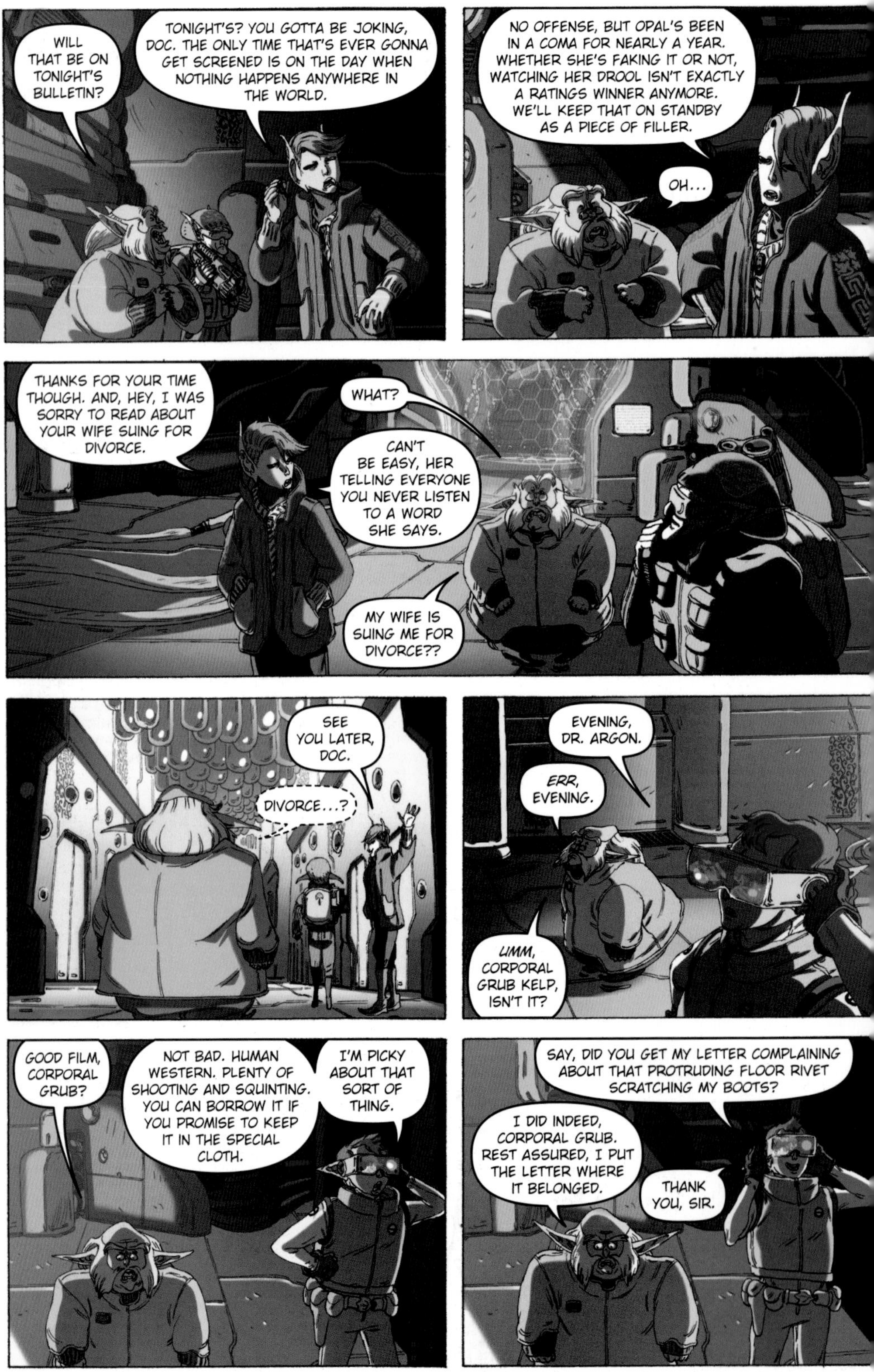
WILL THAT BE ON TONIGHT'S BULLETIN?
TONIGHT'S? YOU GOTTA BE JOKING, DOC. THE ONLY TIME THAT'S EVER GONNA GET SCREENED IS ON THE DAY WHEN NOTHING HAPPENS ANYWHERE IN THE WORLD.
NO OFFENSE, BUT OPAL'S BEEN IN A COMA FOR NEARLY A YEAR. WHETHER SHE'S FAKING IT OR NOT, WATCHING HER DROOL ISN'T EXACTLY A RATINGS WINNER ANYMORE. WE'LL KEEP THAT ON STANDBY AS A PIECE OF FILLER.
OH...
THANKS FOR YOUR TIME THOUGH. AND, HEY, I WAS SORRY TO READ ABOUT YOUR WIFE SUING FOR DIVORCE.
WHAT?
CAN'T BE EASY, HER TELLING EVERYONE YOU NEVER LISTEN TO A WORD SHE SAYS.
MY WIFE IS SUING ME FOR DIVORCE??
SEE YOU LATER, DOC.
DIVORCE...?
EVENING, DR. ARGON.
ERR, EVENING.
UMM, CORPORAL GRUB KELP, ISN'T IT?
GOOD FILM, CORPORAL GRUB?
NOT BAD. HUMAN WESTERN. PLENTY OF SHOOTING AND SQUINTING. YOU CAN BORROW IT IF YOU PROMISE TO KEEP IT IN THE SPECIAL CLOTH.
I'M PICKY ABOUT THAT SORT OF THING.
SAY, DID YOU GET MY LETTER COMPLAINING ABOUT THAT PROTRUDING FLOOR RIVET SCRATCHING MY BOOTS?
I DID INDEED, CORPORAL GRUB. REST ASSURED, I PUT THE LETTER WHERE IT BELONGED.
THANK YOU, SIR.

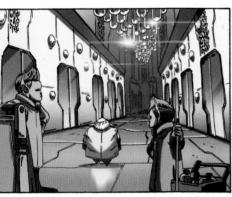

HOW TO RELEASE A DANGEROUS PSYCHOPATH IN TEN EASY STEPS:

STEP 1: ACTIVATE SONIX REMOTE CONTROL.

OKAY, HERE WE GO.

CLICK!

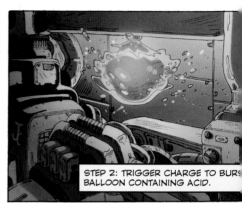

STEP 2: TRIGGER CHARGE TO BURS? BALLOON CONTAINING ACID.

STEP 3: MELT THE CLINIC'S POWER CUBES AND THE BACKUP UNIT.

STEP 4: ENSURE LIGHTS AND ALL SECURITY SYSTEMS ARE OFF-LINE FOR TWO MINUTES.

HEY!

STEP 5: SLIP SEDATIVE PATCH ONTO UNWITTING GUARD.

WHAT'S GOING ON? I'M GONNA...

STEP 6: USE DOOR CODE STOLEN FROM DR. ARGON.

STEP 7: REMOVE SLEEPER TRACER FROM UNDER SKIN. HEAL WOUND WITH MAGIC.

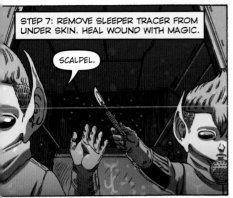

SCALPEL.

STEP 8: WAKE TARGET.

MISS KOBOI?

I'LL JOLT HER.

ZZZZZ

≻GASP≺ CUDGEON!

MISS KOBOI, IT'S US. MERVALL AND DESCANT. IT'S TIME.

"Get the clone."

STEP 9: REPLACE PSYCHOPATH WITH LAB-GROWN CLONE PSYCHOPATH.

IDIOTS. ITS EYES ARE OPEN. IT CAN SEE ME!

DON'T WORRY. IT CAN'T TELL ANYONE.

"But its eyes can register images. Foaly may think to check."

"Don't fret, miss. Very soon, that will be the least of Foaly's worries."

STEP 10: IMPLANT SLEEPER TRACER IN CLONE. HEAL WOUND WITH MAGIC.

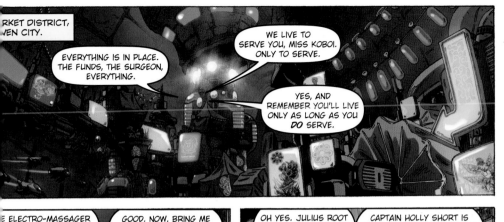

RKET DISTRICT,
VEN CITY.

EVERYTHING IS IN PLACE. THE FUNDS, THE SURGEON, EVERYTHING.

WE LIVE TO SERVE YOU, MISS KOBOI. ONLY TO SERVE.

YES, AND REMEMBER YOU'LL LIVE ONLY AS LONG AS YOU *DO* SERVE.

E ELECTRO-MASSAGER L HAVE YOUR MUSCLES ACK TO NORMAL IN A FEW DAYS, MISS.

GOOD. NOW, BRING ME UP TO SPEED. MY ENEMIES ARE WELL AND HAPPY, I TRUST?

OH YES. JULIUS ROOT GOES FROM STRENGTH TO STRENGTH. HE HAS BEEN NOMINATED FOR THE COUNCIL.

CAPTAIN HOLLY SHORT IS BACK ON ACTIVE DUTY. MANY SUCCESSFUL RECONNAISSANCE MISSIONS SINCE YOU INDUCED YOUR OWN COMA. UP FOR PROMOTION TO MAJOR.

CENTAUR, FOALY, IS OBNOXIOUS AS EVER. I SUGGEST—

TWICE IN MY LIFE SOMEONE HAS OUTSMARTED ME. BOTH TIMES IT WAS FOALY.

NOTHING HAPPENS TO FOALY YET.

HE WILL BE DEFEATED BY INTELLECT ALONE. I WANT HIM UTTERLY HUMILIATED.

OH, AND PASS ME A MIRROR.

AS FOR THE HUMAN, ARTEMIS FOWL. HE HAS SPENT MUCH OF THE LAST YEAR TRYING TO FIND A PARTICULAR PAINTING. WE HAVE TRACED THE PAINTING TO MUNICH.

REALLY? THEN LET'S MAKE SURE THAT WE GET TO IT BEFORE HE DOES.

MAYBE WE CAN ADD A LITTLE SOMETHING TO HIS WORK OF ART.

I WILL HAVE MY REVENGE ON ALL OF THEM. NOW, LET'S GET STARTED. SUMMON THE SURGEON.

I WONDER, WHAT WILL I LOOK LIKE AS A HUMAN?

Thieves have their own folklore.

Stories of ingenious heists and death-defying robberies.

Perhaps the most thrilling legend is the tale of the lost Hervé masterpiece.

CHAPTER 2:
THE FAIRY THIE[F]

Every schoolboy knows that Pascal Hervé was the French Impressionist who painted extraordinarily beautiful pictures of the fairy folk.

And every art dealer knows that Hervé's fifteen fairy paintings command sums of over 50 million Euros each.

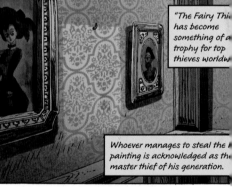

In the upper criminal echelons there were always rumors of a secret, final, sixteenth painting. Entitled "The Fairy Thief," it is said to depict a fairy in the act of stealing a human child.

Legend has it that Hervé gav[e] the painting to [a] beautiful Turki[sh] girl he met on [the] Champs-Élysé[es].

The girl promptly broke Hervé's heart and sold the picture to an English tourist for twenty francs. Within weeks, the picture had been stolen from the Englishman's home.

Since that time, it's believed the painting has been stolen fifteen times. What is unique is that each time the thief decided to keep the painting.

"The Fairy Thie[f]" has become something of a trophy for top thieves worldw[ide].

Whoever manages to steal the [painting] painting is acknowledged as the master thief of his generation.

I am Artemis Fowl the Second.

I am fourteen years old. I am a genius.

For as long as I can remember, I have been fascinated by fair[ies]. I do not know why.

If I succeed, I will be the [youngest] youngest thief to have ev[er] stolen "The Fairy Thief."

If:

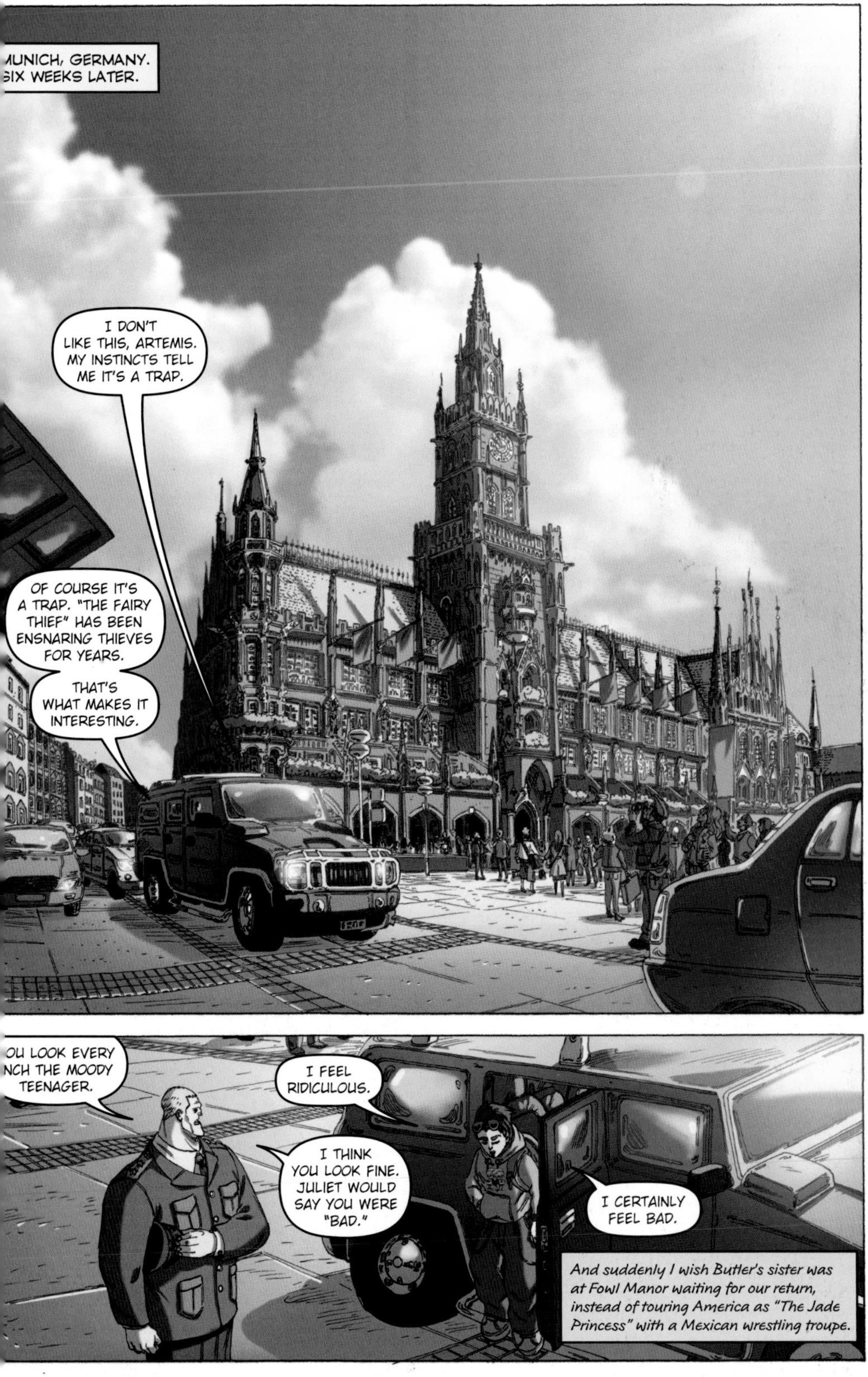
MUNICH, GERMANY. SIX WEEKS LATER.
I DON'T LIKE THIS, ARTEMIS. MY INSTINCTS TELL ME IT'S A TRAP.
OF COURSE IT'S A TRAP. "THE FAIRY THIEF" HAS BEEN ENSNARING THIEVES FOR YEARS.
THAT'S WHAT MAKES IT INTERESTING.
OU LOOK EVERY NCH THE MOODY TEENAGER.
I FEEL RIDICULOUS.
I THINK YOU LOOK FINE. JULIET WOULD SAY YOU WERE "BAD."
I CERTAINLY FEEL BAD.
And suddenly I wish Butler's sister was at Fowl Manor waiting for our return, instead of touring America as "The Jade Princess" with a Mexican wrestling troupe.

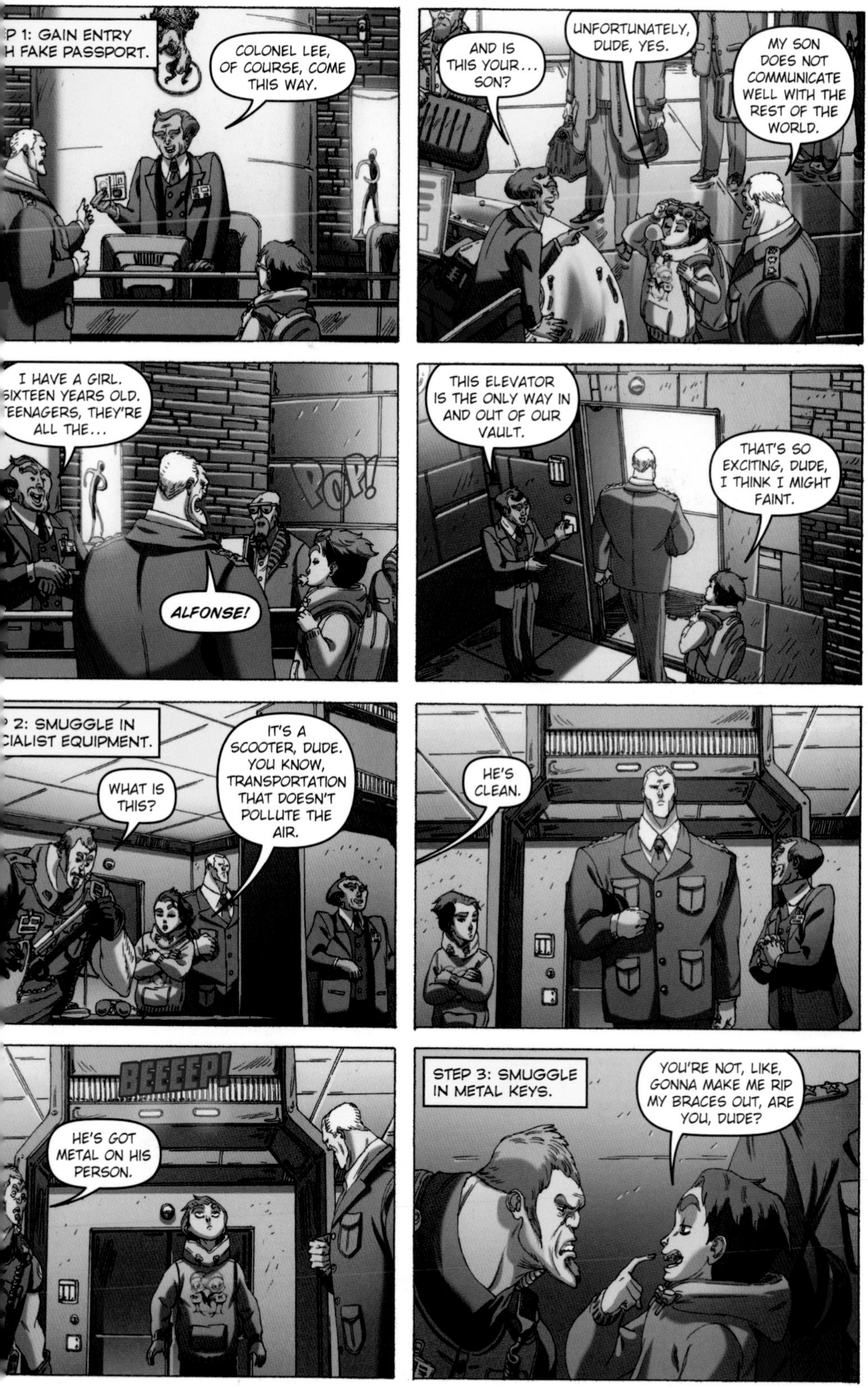

P 1: GAIN ENTRY
H FAKE PASSPORT.
COLONEL LEE, OF COURSE, COME THIS WAY.
AND IS THIS YOUR... SON?
UNFORTUNATELY, DUDE, YES.
MY SON DOES NOT COMMUNICATE WELL WITH THE REST OF THE WORLD.
I HAVE A GIRL. SIXTEEN YEARS OLD. TEENAGERS, THEY'RE ALL THE...
POP!
ALFONSE!
THIS ELEVATOR IS THE ONLY WAY IN AND OUT OF OUR VAULT.
THAT'S SO EXCITING, DUDE, I THINK I MIGHT FAINT.
P 2: SMUGGLE IN
CIALIST EQUIPMENT.
WHAT IS THIS?
IT'S A SCOOTER, DUDE. YOU KNOW, TRANSPORTATION THAT DOESN'T POLLUTE THE AIR.
HE'S CLEAN.
BEEEEP!
HE'S GOT METAL ON HIS PERSON.
STEP 3: SMUGGLE IN METAL KEYS.
YOU'RE NOT, LIKE, GONNA MAKE ME RIP MY BRACES OUT, ARE YOU, DUDE?

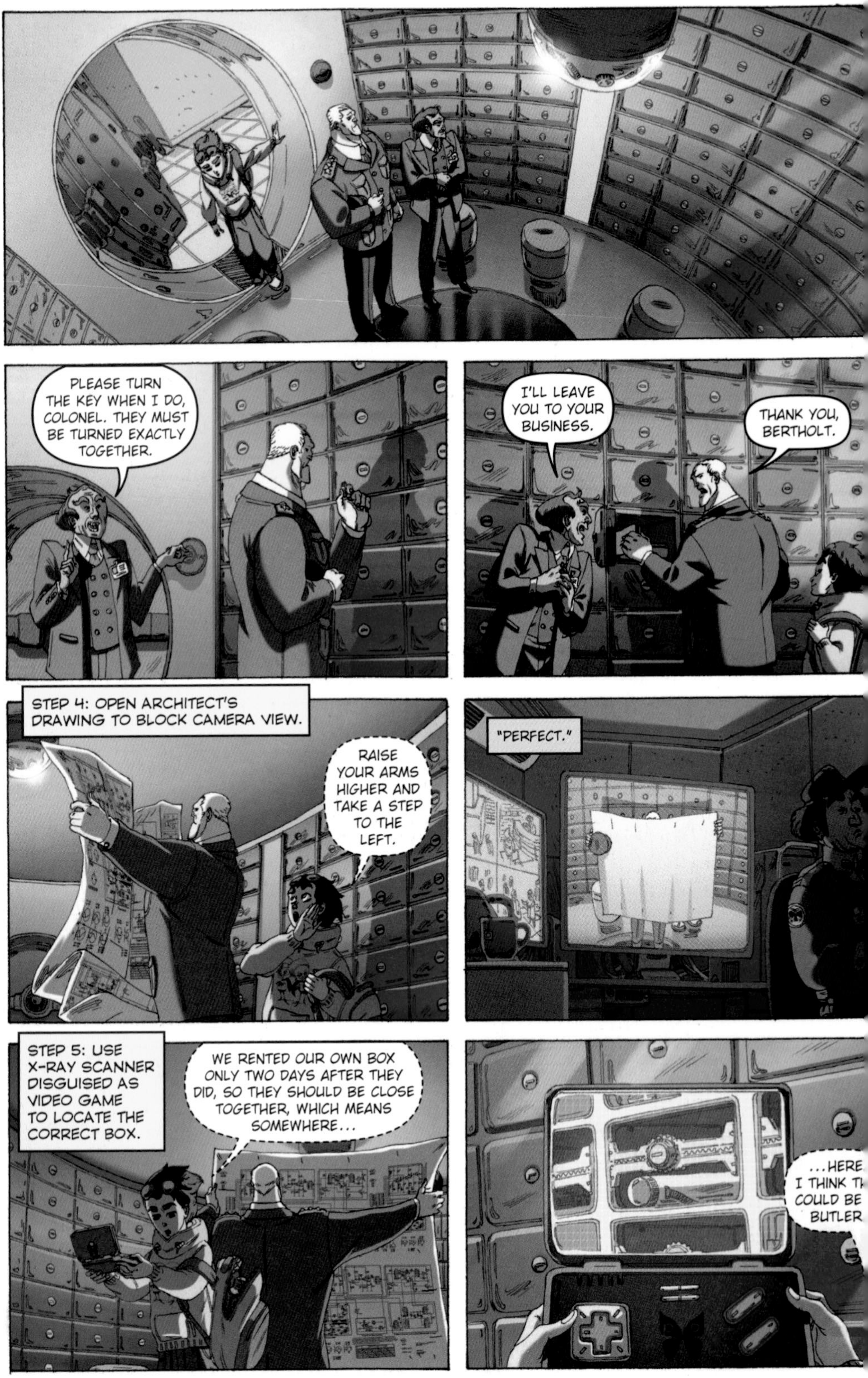
PLEASE TURN THE KEY WHEN I DO, COLONEL. THEY MUST BE TURNED EXACTLY TOGETHER.
I'LL LEAVE YOU TO YOUR BUSINESS.
THANK YOU, BERTHOLT.
STEP 4: OPEN ARCHITECT'S DRAWING TO BLOCK CAMERA VIEW.
RAISE YOUR ARMS HIGHER AND TAKE A STEP TO THE LEFT.
"PERFECT."
STEP 5: USE X-RAY SCANNER DISGUISED AS VIDEO GAME TO LOCATE THE CORRECT BOX.
WE RENTED OUR OWN BOX ONLY TWO DAYS AFTER THEY DID, SO THEY SHOULD BE CLOSE TOGETHER, WHICH MEANS SOMEWHERE...
...HERE
I THINK T
COULD BE
BUTLER

STEP 6: LOCATE THE
LOCKSMITH'S SIGNATURE.

STEP 7: RETRIEVE
MASTER KEYS
ALLOWED THROUGH
METAL DETECTOR.

STEP 8: USE SPECIALLY
ADAPTED SCOOTER COLUMN TO
TURN TWO KEYS AT SAME TIME.

HERE
WE GO...

YES!

AMAZING HOW THE TIGHTEST ELECTRONIC
SECURITY CAN BE DEFEATED BY A POLE,
A PULLEY, AND A BRACE.

CLICK

STEP 9: CHECK DEPOSIT
BOX FOR BOOBY TRAPS.

HA—A CIRCUIT
BREAKER ATTACHED
TO A PORTABLE
KLAXON.

HOW
EMBARRASSING
FOR ANY THIEF TO
GET CAUGHT LIKE
THAT. SOMEONE
HAS A SENSE OF
HUMOR.

STEP 10:
DISCONNECT
BOOBY TRAP.

ARE WE
DONE, ARTEMIS?
MY ARMS ARE
GETTING RATHER
TIRED.

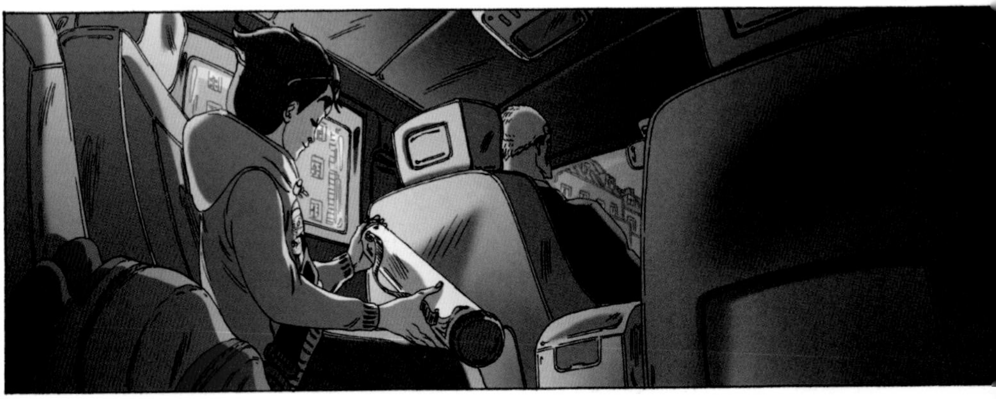

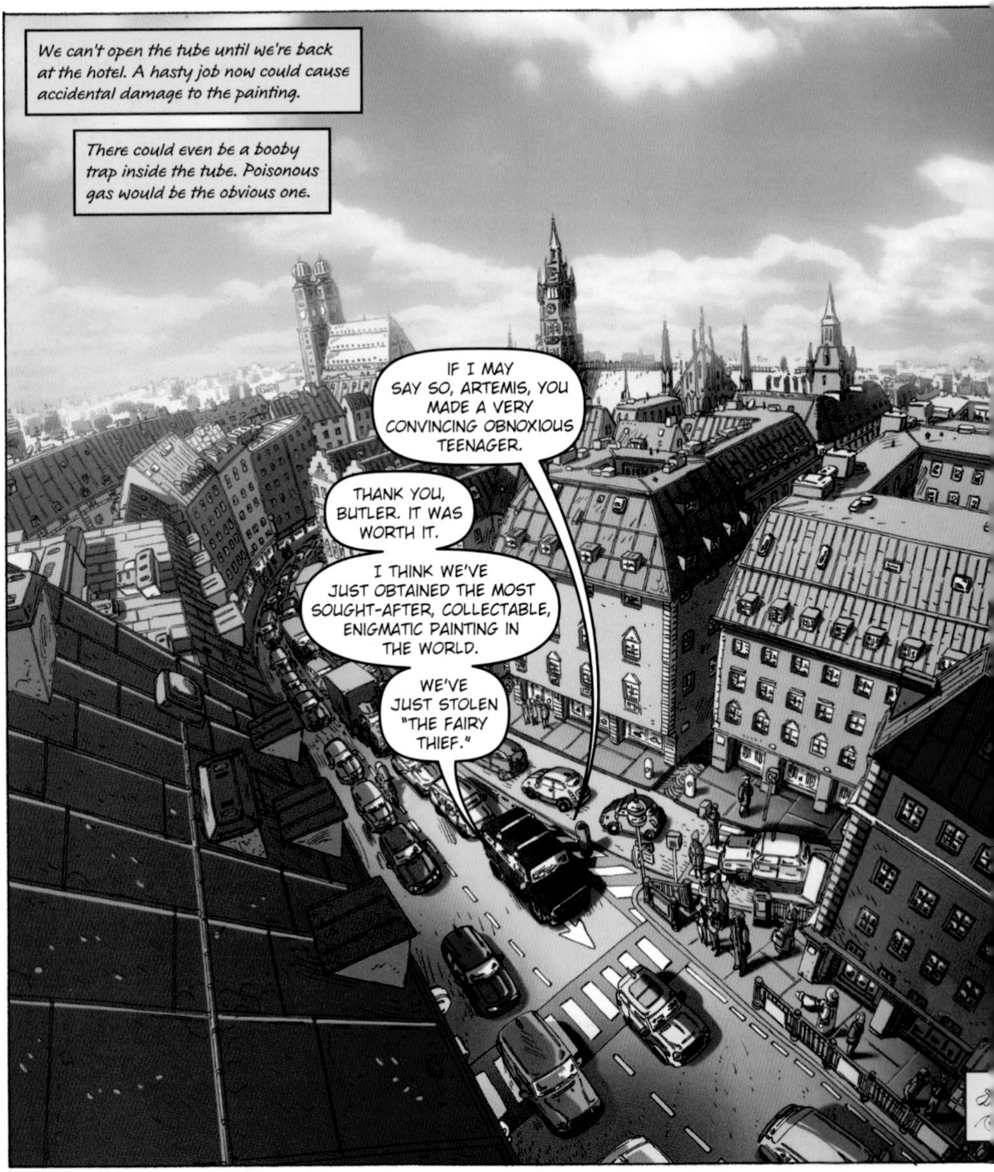

We can't open the tube until we're back at the hotel. A hasty job now could cause accidental damage to the painting.
There could even be a booby trap inside the tube. Poisonous gas would be the obvious one.
IF I MAY SAY SO, ARTEMIS, YOU MADE A VERY CONVINCING OBNOXIOUS TEENAGER.
THANK YOU, BUTLER. IT WAS WORTH IT.
I THINK WE'VE JUST OBTAINED THE MOST SOUGHT-AFTER, COLLECTABLE, ENIGMATIC PAINTING IN THE WORLD.
WE'VE JUST STOLEN "THE FAIRY THIEF."

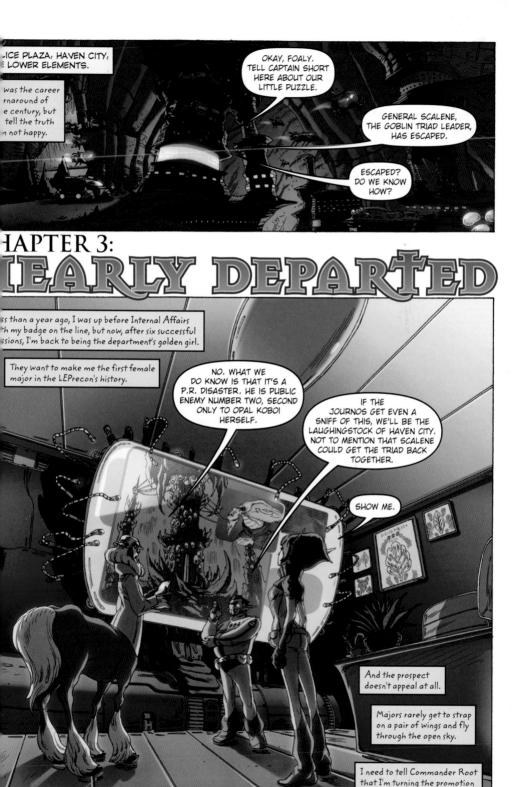

ICE PLAZA, HAVEN CITY,
LOWER ELEMENTS.

was the career
rnaround of
e century, but
tell the truth
n not happy.

OKAY, FOALY.
TELL CAPTAIN SHORT
HERE ABOUT OUR
LITTLE PUZZLE.

GENERAL SCALENE,
THE GOBLIN TRIAD LEADER,
HAS ESCAPED.

ESCAPED?
DO WE KNOW
HOW?

HAPTER 3:

EARLY DEPARTED

ss than a year ago, I was up before Internal Affairs
th my badge on the line, but now, after six successful
ssions, I'm back to being the department's golden girl.

They want to make me the first female
major in the LEPrecon's history.

NO. WHAT WE
DO KNOW IS THAT IT'S A
P.R. DISASTER. HE IS PUBLIC
ENEMY NUMBER TWO, SECOND
ONLY TO OPAL KOBOI
HERSELF.

IF THE
JOURNOS GET EVEN A
SNIFF OF THIS, WE'LL BE THE
LAUGHINGSTOCK OF HAVEN CITY.
NOT TO MENTION THAT SCALENE
COULD GET THE TRIAD BACK
TOGETHER.

SHOW ME.

And the prospect
doesn't appeal at all.

Majors rarely get to strap
on a pair of wings and fly
through the open sky.

I need to tell Commander Root
that I'm turning the promotion
down. But right now there is
police work to be done.

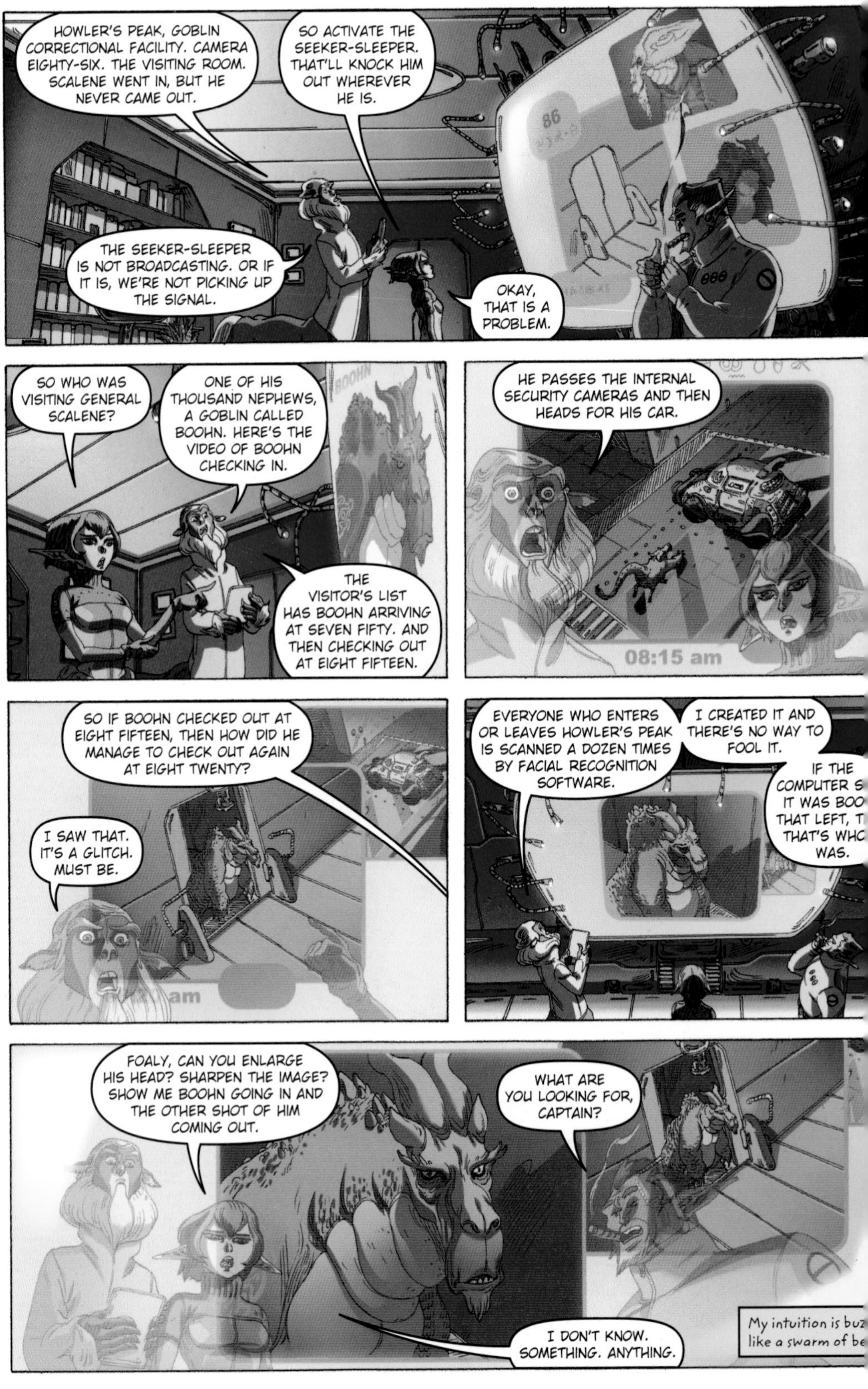

HOWLER'S PEAK, GOBLIN CORRECTIONAL FACILITY. CAMERA EIGHTY-SIX. THE VISITING ROOM. SCALENE WENT IN, BUT HE NEVER CAME OUT.
SO ACTIVATE THE SEEKER-SLEEPER. THAT'LL KNOCK HIM OUT WHEREVER HE IS.
THE SEEKER-SLEEPER IS NOT BROADCASTING. OR IF IT IS, WE'RE NOT PICKING UP THE SIGNAL.
OKAY, THAT IS A PROBLEM.
SO WHO WAS VISITING GENERAL SCALENE?
ONE OF HIS THOUSAND NEPHEWS, A GOBLIN CALLED BOOHN. HERE'S THE VIDEO OF BOOHN CHECKING IN.
THE VISITOR'S LIST HAS BOOHN ARRIVING AT SEVEN FIFTY. AND THEN CHECKING OUT AT EIGHT FIFTEEN.
HE PASSES THE INTERNAL SECURITY CAMERAS AND THEN HEADS FOR HIS CAR.
08:15 am
SO IF BOOHN CHECKED OUT AT EIGHT FIFTEEN, THEN HOW DID HE MANAGE TO CHECK OUT AGAIN AT EIGHT TWENTY?
I SAW THAT. IT'S A GLITCH. MUST BE.
EVERYONE WHO ENTERS OR LEAVES HOWLER'S PEAK IS SCANNED A DOZEN TIMES BY FACIAL RECOGNITION SOFTWARE.
I CREATED IT AND THERE'S NO WAY TO FOOL IT.
IF THE COMPUTER S IT WAS BOO THAT LEFT, T THAT'S WHO WAS.
FOALY, CAN YOU ENLARGE HIS HEAD? SHARPEN THE IMAGE? SHOW ME BOOHN GOING IN AND THE OTHER SHOT OF HIM COMING OUT.
WHAT ARE YOU LOOKING FOR, CAPTAIN?
I DON'T KNOW. SOMETHING. ANYTHING.
My intuition is buz like a swarm of be

"...ook, here's
scale blister.
...ow look at
...e exit film.
...o blister."

"So, he burst
the blister.
Big deal."

"No, it's more
than that."

GOING IN, BOOHN'S SKIN IS
ALMOST GREY. COMING OUT
HE'S BRIGHT GREEN.

WHAT'S
YOUR POINT,
CAPTAIN?

BOOHN SHED
HIS SKIN IN THE
VISITOR'S ROOM.
SO WHERE'S
THE SKIN?

Foaly pulls up footage
of the first "Boohn"
leaving the visitor's
room. It looks a lot
like Boohn, but at
high magnification it's
clear that the goblin's
skin is ill-fitting.

Patches are
missing and the
goblin seems to
be holding folds
together.

...HIS WAS ALL PLANNED.
...OOHN WAITS UNTIL HE'S
...HEDDING. THEN HE VISITS
...S UNCLE AND THEY PEEL
OFF HIS SKIN.

GENERAL SCALENE
PUTS ON THE SKIN AND
JUST WALKS OUT THE
DOOR, FOOLING FOALY'S
AUTOMATIC SCANNERS
ON THE WAY.

WE NEED
TO CATCH SCALENE
AND FIND OUT WHO
PLANNED THIS.

WHOEVER
IT IS, AT LEAST IT'S
NOT OPAL. THIS IS A
LIVE FEED AND SHE'S
STILL IN DREAMY
DREAMLAND.

...IR. MAJOR KELP REPORTS
...HAT HE'S LOCATED GENERAL
SCALENE.

HE'S IN
CHUTE E37, SIR.
AND HE'S ASKING
FOR YOU.

WHAT?

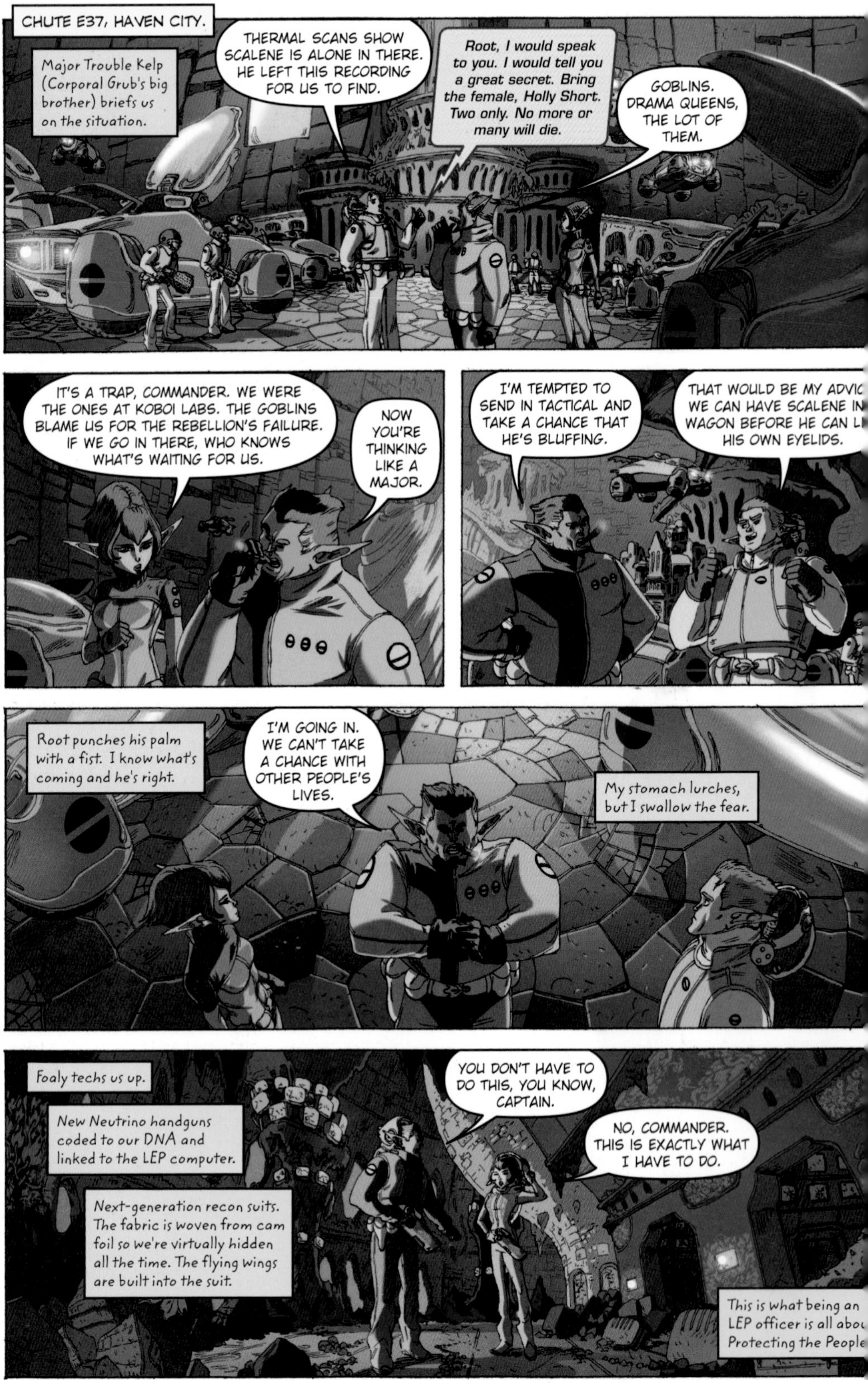
CHUTE E37, HAVEN CITY.
Major Trouble Kelp (Corporal Grub's big brother) briefs us on the situation.
THERMAL SCANS SHOW SCALENE IS ALONE IN THERE. HE LEFT THIS RECORDING FOR US TO FIND.
Root, I would speak to you. I would tell you a great secret. Bring the female, Holly Short. Two only. No more or many will die.
GOBLINS. DRAMA QUEENS, THE LOT OF THEM.
IT'S A TRAP, COMMANDER. WE WERE THE ONES AT KOBOI LABS. THE GOBLINS BLAME US FOR THE REBELLION'S FAILURE. IF WE GO IN THERE, WHO KNOWS WHAT'S WAITING FOR US.
NOW YOU'RE THINKING LIKE A MAJOR.
I'M TEMPTED TO SEND IN TACTICAL AND TAKE A CHANCE THAT HE'S BLUFFING.
THAT WOULD BE MY ADVIC WE CAN HAVE SCALENE IN WAGON BEFORE HE CAN LI HIS OWN EYELIDS.
Root punches his palm with a fist. I know what's coming and he's right.
I'M GOING IN. WE CAN'T TAKE A CHANCE WITH OTHER PEOPLE'S LIVES.
My stomach lurches, but I swallow the fear.
Foaly techs us up.
New Neutrino handguns coded to our DNA and linked to the LEP computer.
Next-generation recon suits. The fabric is woven from cam foil so we're virtually hidden all the time. The flying wings are built into the suit.
YOU DON'T HAVE TO DO THIS, YOU KNOW, CAPTAIN.
NO, COMMANDER. THIS IS EXACTLY WHAT I HAVE TO DO.
This is what being an LEP officer is all abou Protecting the People

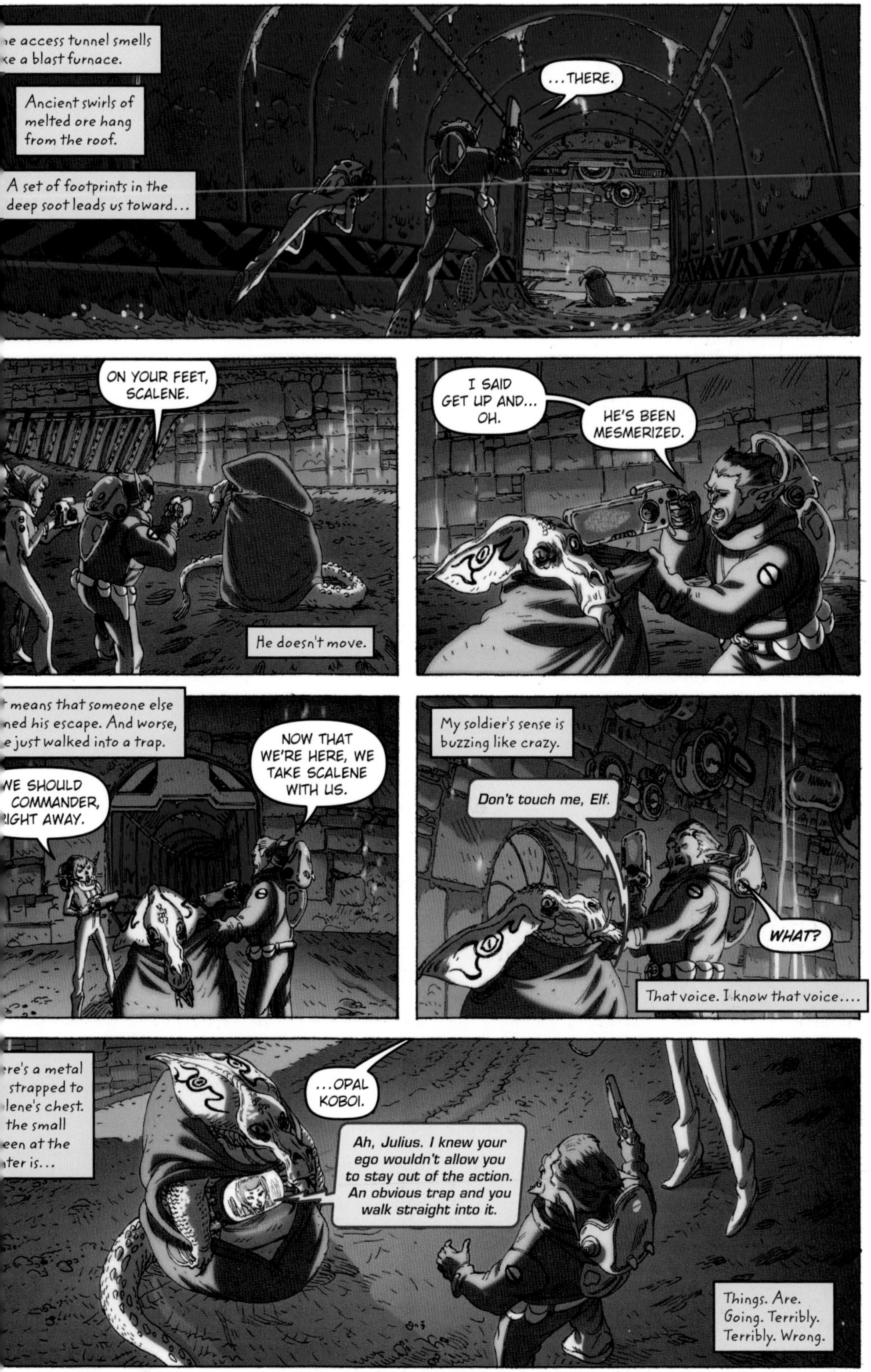
e access tunnel smells
e a blast furnace.
Ancient swirls of melted ore hang from the roof.
A set of footprints in the deep soot leads us toward...
...THERE.
ON YOUR FEET, SCALENE.
He doesn't move.
I SAID GET UP AND... OH.
HE'S BEEN MESMERIZED.
means that someone else
ned his escape. And worse,
e just walked into a trap.
NOW THAT WE'RE HERE, WE TAKE SCALENE WITH US.
E SHOULD
COMMANDER,
IGHT AWAY.
My soldier's sense is buzzing like crazy.
Don't touch me, Elf.
WHAT?
That voice. I know that voice....
re's a metal
strapped to
lene's chest.
the small
een at the
ter is...
...OPAL KOBOI.
Ah, Julius. I knew your ego wouldn't allow you to stay out of the action. An obvious trap and you walk straight into it.
Things. Are. Going. Terribly. Terribly. Wrong.

FOALY, WE HAVE A SITUATION HERE. *OPAL KOBOI IS LOOSE!* I REPEAT, LOOSE. PUT OUT A CITYWIDE ALERT. *FOALY?*

Talk all you want, Captain Short. Foaly can't hear you. My device is blocking your transmissions as I blocked your seeker-sleeper earlier.

I point my helmet camera. Foaly will see it's her and work out the rest.

Oh, very good, Captai You were always a smart Relatively speaking, of co

Sorry to disappoint you, but thi entire device is made of stealth o and is practically invisible. All Foaly see is a slight shimmer of interfere

The blast doors slam shut behind us.

WE'RE COMPLETELY CUT OFF FROM THE LEP.

SLAMMM!

Alone at last.

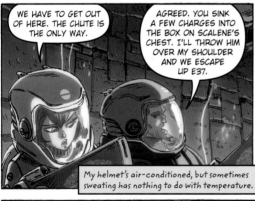

WE HAVE TO GET OUT OF HERE. THE CHUTE IS THE ONLY WAY.

AGREED. YOU SINK A FEW CHARGES INTO THE BOX ON SCALENE'S CHEST. I'LL THROW HIM OVER MY SHOULDER AND WE ESCAPE UP E37.

My helmet's air-conditioned, but sometimes sweating has nothing to do with temperature.

I can't help but wonder, is this exactly what Opal wants us to do?

Have we come up with a little plan to...

BDAM BDAM BDAM!

Root leans down and grabs Scalene. Nothing happens. Maybe I'm wrong. Maybe Opal has no plan.

Then suddenly, the octo-bonds holding the screen let go of Scalene and whiplash around Commander Root.

AGGGH!

Looks like you're the sacrifice, Commander Root.

D'ARVIT!

I hear a rib crack. Blue sparks of magic start to heal it.

I move to help, but there's an urgent beeping from the device.

STAY BACK; IT'S A PROXIMITY TRIGGER.

Listen to him, Captain Short. If you come too close, he will be vaporized by the explosives now strapped to his chest.

—OALY'S WATCHING S. HE'LL FIND US A WAY OUT."

"Ha—Foaly **is** watching and probably wondering why you're pointing a gun at your commanding officer. Remember Foaly can't hear anything and he can't see my screen."

A digital readout flicks into life on Root's chest. A six and a zero.

Once I start the countdown, you have one minute to live, Commander. How does that feel?

—al's snide laugh —lls into my brain.

SHUT IT DOWN, KOBOI. OR I SWEAR I'LL...

Root is already dead. At least save the Mud Men?

Mud Men? Of course. Artemis and Butler. The two other people who helped stop Koboi's plan.

At this very moment, young Artemis is stealing a package from the International Bank in Munich.

He believes it contains a valuable painting. It does. It also contains a homing chip for a bio-bomb.

"You can stay —re and attempt — explain all this. — shouldn't take —ore than a few —urs. Or you can —y to keep your —riends alive."

I WILL HUNT YOU DOWN, KOBOI. FOR YOU, THERE WON'T BE A SAFE INCH ON THE PLANET.

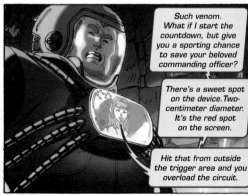

Such venom. What if I start the countdown, but give you a sporting chance to save your beloved commanding officer?

There's a sweet spot on the device. Two-centimeter diameter. It's the red spot on the screen.

Hit that from outside the trigger area and you overload the circuit.

She's lying. But I can't take the chance she's not.

DON'T TAKE THE SHOT. JUST GET OUT OF RANGE. GO AND SAVE ARTEMIS.

THAT'S THE LAST ORDER I'LL EVER GIVE YOU, CAPTAIN. DON'T YOU DARE IGNORE IT.

There are already tears in my eyes.

I DON'T HAVE ANY CHOICE, JULIUS.

DON'T CALL ME JULIU YOU ALWAYS DO THAT J BEFORE YOU DISOBEY SAVE ARTEMIS.

I'LL SAVE ARTEMIS NEXT.

I take a deep breath, hold it, then pull the trigger.

BDAM!

I'm certain I hit the spot. But the countdown on Root's chest goes into overdrive.

I think you were a fraction low. Hard luck. I mean that sincerely.

NO!

Commander Root looks straight at me. His eyes are steady and fearless.

HOLLY...

BE WELL.

An orange flame star to blossom in the cent of his chest. No, pleas

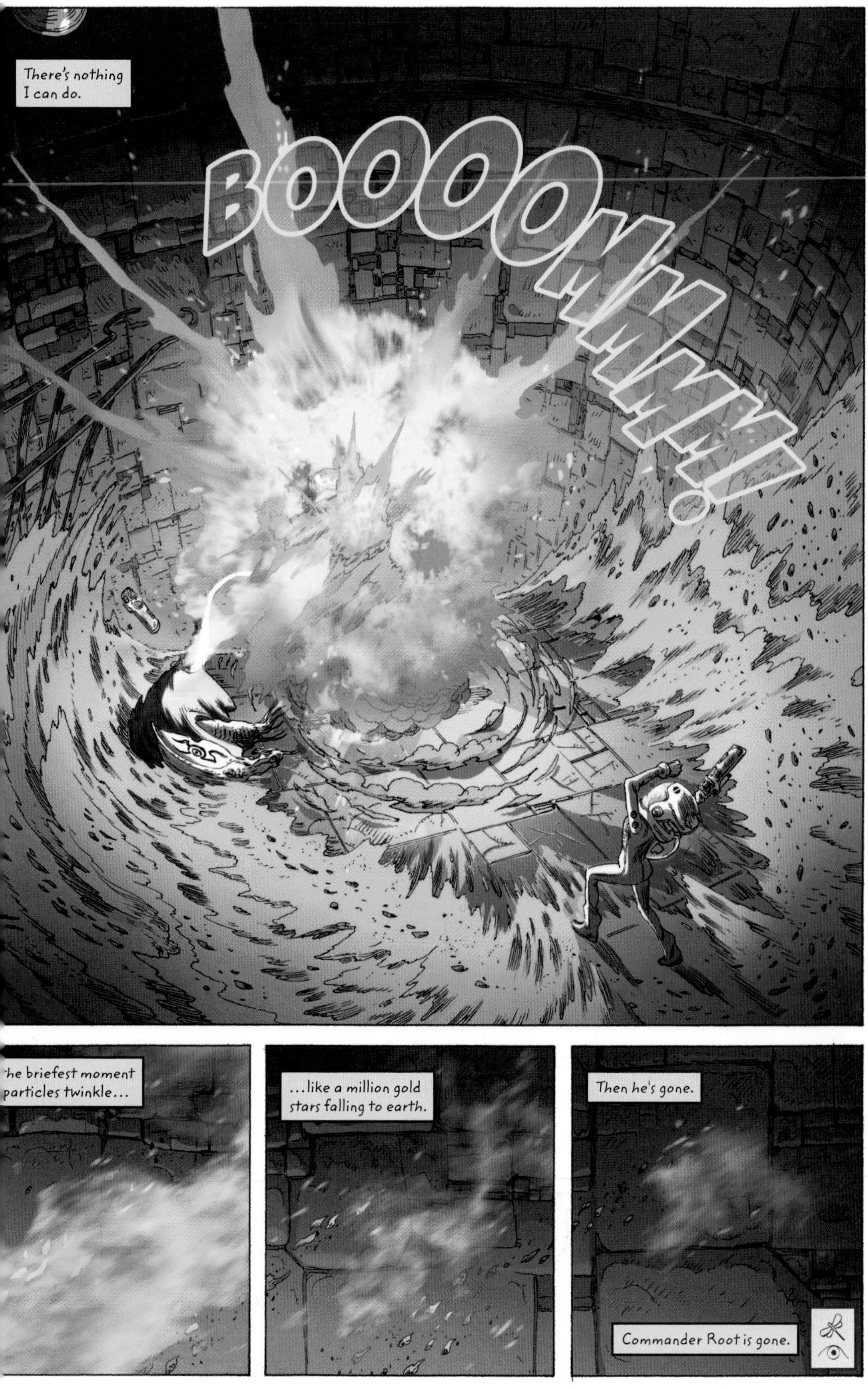
There's nothing I can do.
BOOOOMMMM!!
he briefest moment particles twinkle...
...like a million gold stars falling to earth.
Then he's gone.
Commander Root is gone.

COMMANDER ROOT

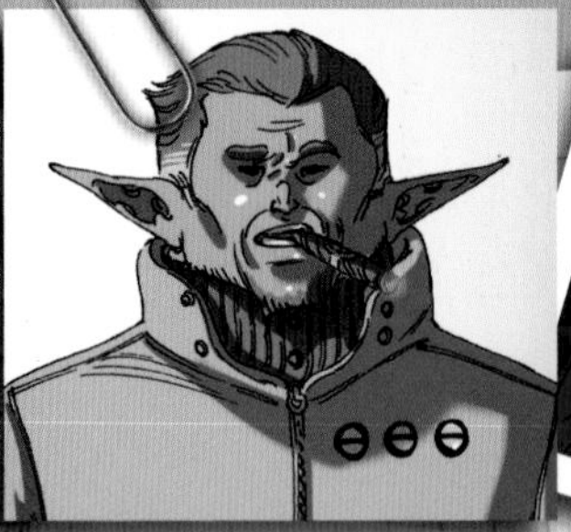

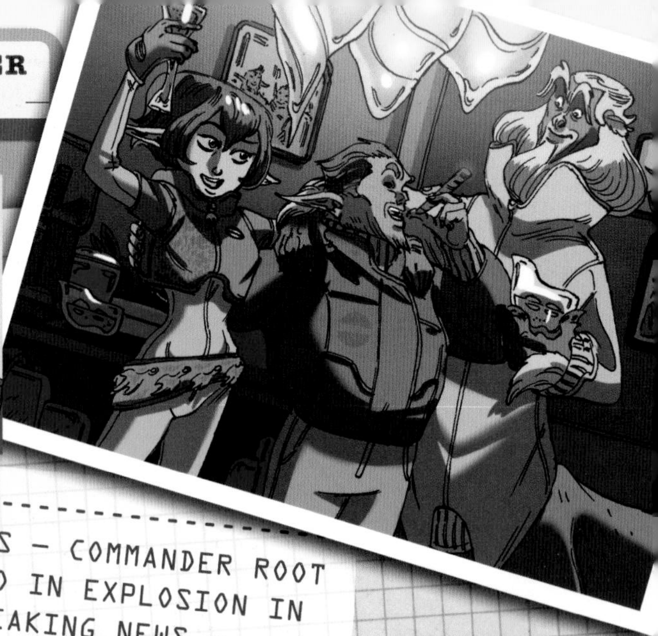

- BREAKING NEWS - COMMANDER ROOT BELIEVED KILLED IN EXPLOSION IN CHUTE E37 - BREAKING NEWS -

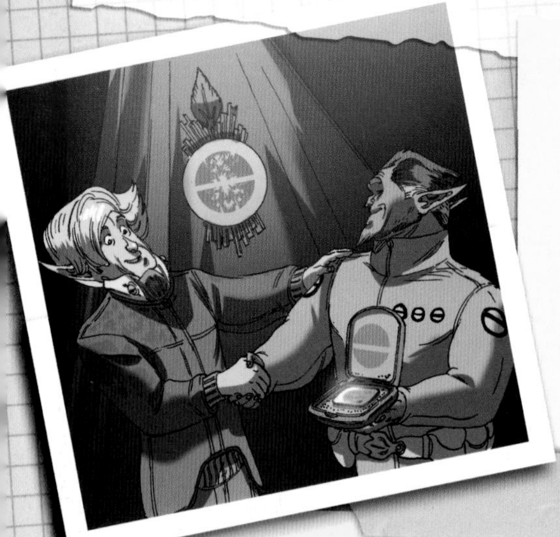

—MEMO—

FROM: EDITOR IN CHIEF
TO: NEWSROOM STAFF

If this terrible news is true then we're going to need wall-to-wall coverage of this tragic (and potenti[ally] ratings-increasing) event.

TO-DO LIST

1. Get a camera crew over to chute E37 and another to Police Plaza.
2. Pull all archive files on Commander Root and his decades in charge of the LEP recon unit.
3. Find out who sold him those noxious fungus cigars and interview them—adds character.
4. Avoid all mention of his brother, Turnball Root. Best not to drag that low-life criminal into this story. Keep it heroic.
5. Why are you still reading this? Get out there and get me this story!
6. Err . . . And find out how he died!?

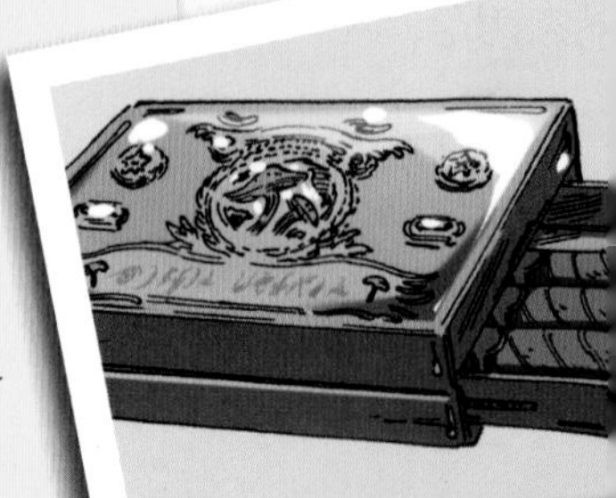

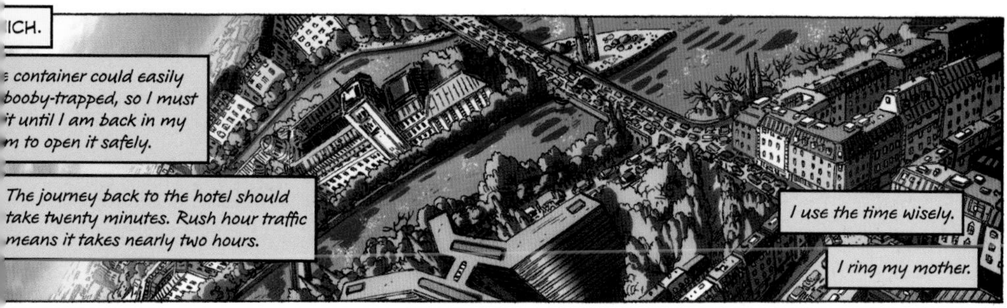
ICH.
: container could easily
booby-trapped, so I must
'it until I am back in my
m to open it safely.
The journey back to the hotel should
take twenty minutes. Rush hour traffic
means it takes nearly two hours.
I use the time wisely.
I ring my mother.

IAPTER 4:
IARROW ESCAPES

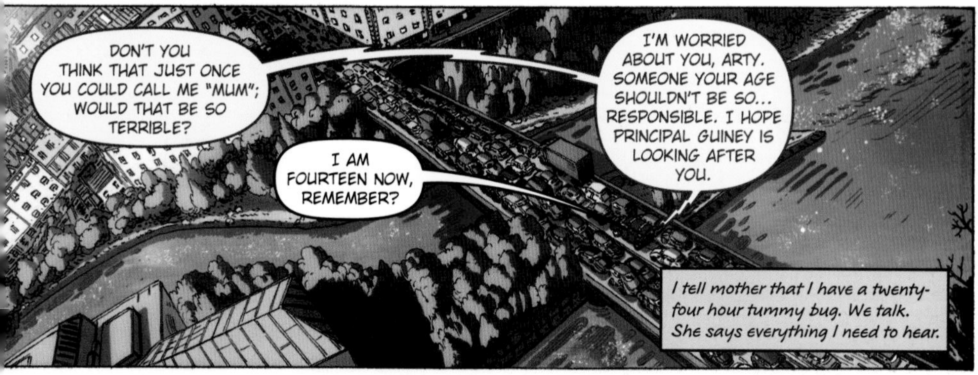
DON'T YOU THINK THAT JUST ONCE YOU COULD CALL ME "MUM"; WOULD THAT BE SO TERRIBLE?
I'M WORRIED ABOUT YOU, ARTY. SOMEONE YOUR AGE SHOULDN'T BE SO... RESPONSIBLE. I HOPE PRINCIPAL GUINEY IS LOOKING AFTER YOU.
I AM FOURTEEN NOW, REMEMBER?
I tell mother that I have a twenty-four hour tummy bug. We talk. She says everything I need to hear.

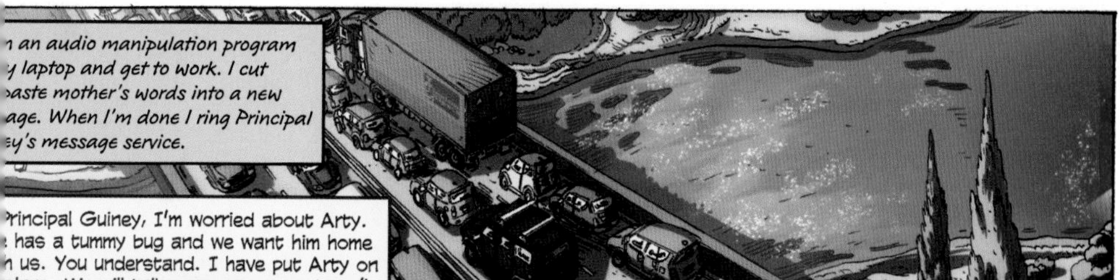
n an audio manipulation program
y laptop and get to work. I cut
paste mother's words into a new
age. When I'm done I ring Principal
ey's message service.
Principal Guiney, I'm worried about Arty.
: has a tummy bug and we want him home
n us. You understand. I have put Arty on
plane. We will talk more on your return."
That takes care of school for a few days.

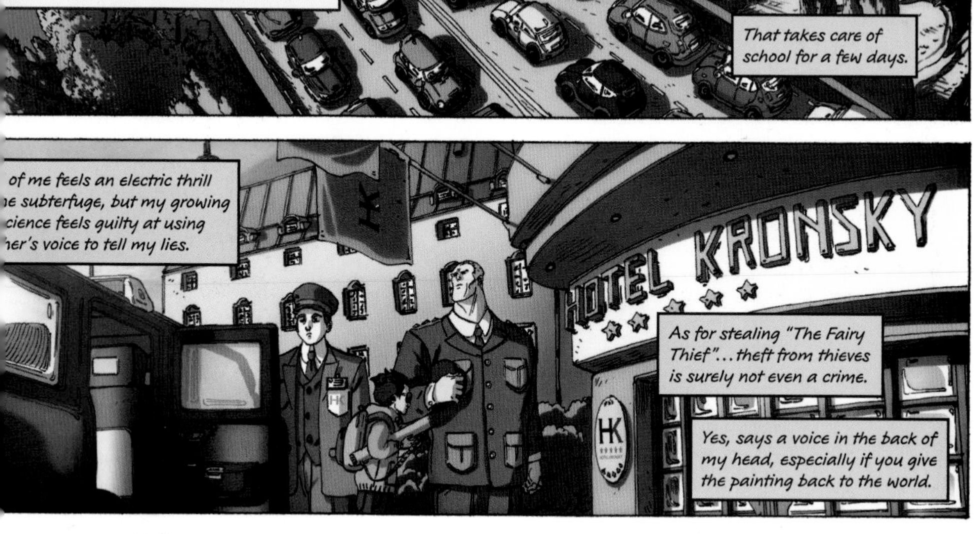
of me feels an electric thrill
e subterfuge, but my growing
cience feels guilty at using
her's voice to tell my lies.
HOTEL KRONSKY
As for stealing "The Fairy Thief"...theft from thieves is surely not even a crime.
Yes, says a voice in the back of my head, especially if you give the painting back to the world.

In the privacy of my hotel room, I get to work.

The first task is to check the container for poison gas.

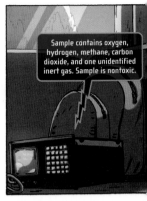

Sample contains oxygen, hydrogen, methane, carbon dioxide, and one unidentified inert gas. Sample is nontoxic.

I tease the painting from the cylinder and unroll it.

The figures are painted so beautifully they seem to sparkle.

I know immediately... this is no fake.

THE FAIRY CAN'T GO INSIDE....

The fairy is perched on the windowsill because it can't go inside without an invitation.

How do I know that?

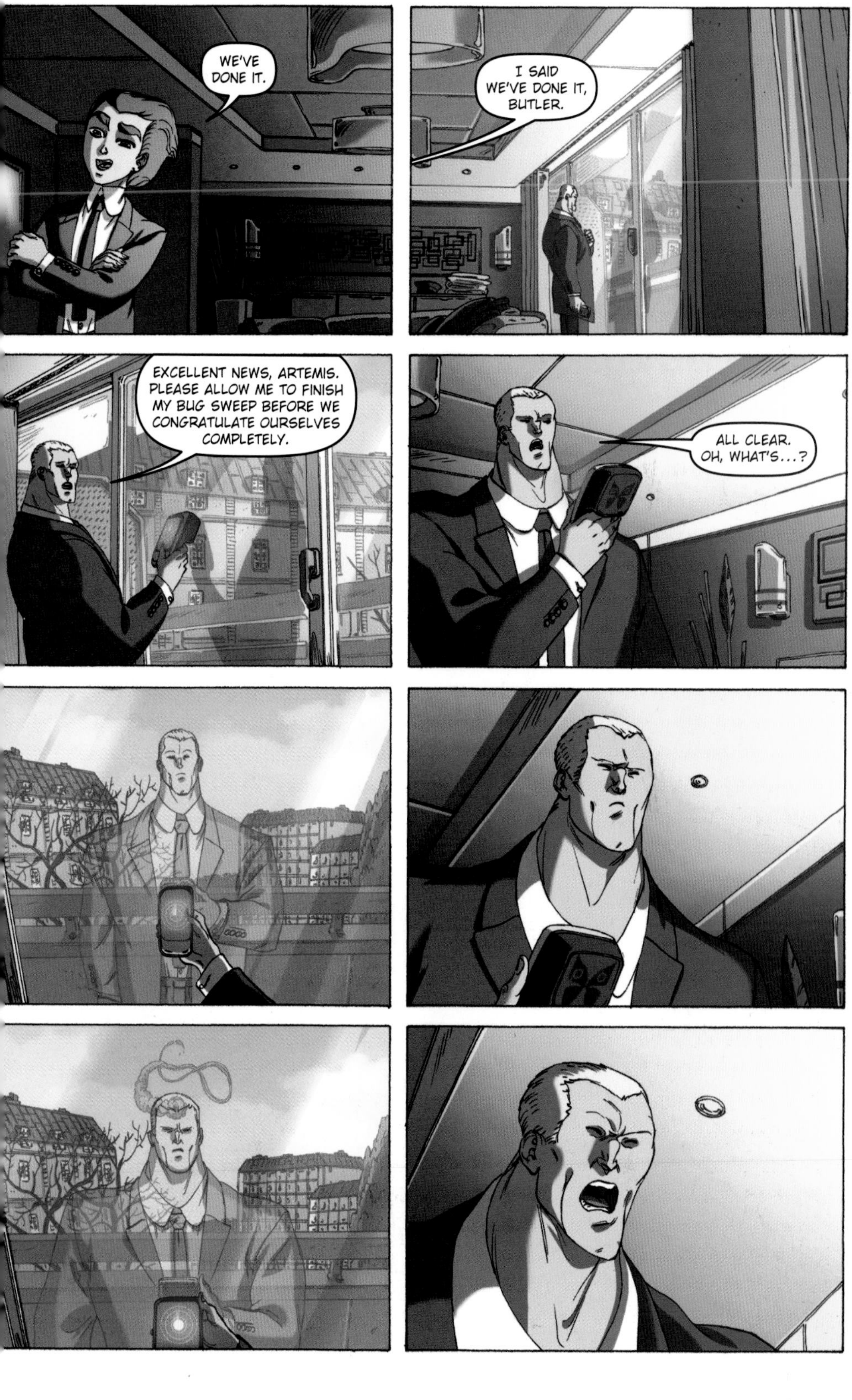
WE'VE DONE IT.
I SAID WE'VE DONE IT, BUTLER.
EXCELLENT NEWS, ARTEMIS. PLEASE ALLOW ME TO FINISH MY BUG SWEEP BEFORE WE CONGRATULATE OURSELVES COMPLETELY.
ALL CLEAR. OH, WHAT'S...?

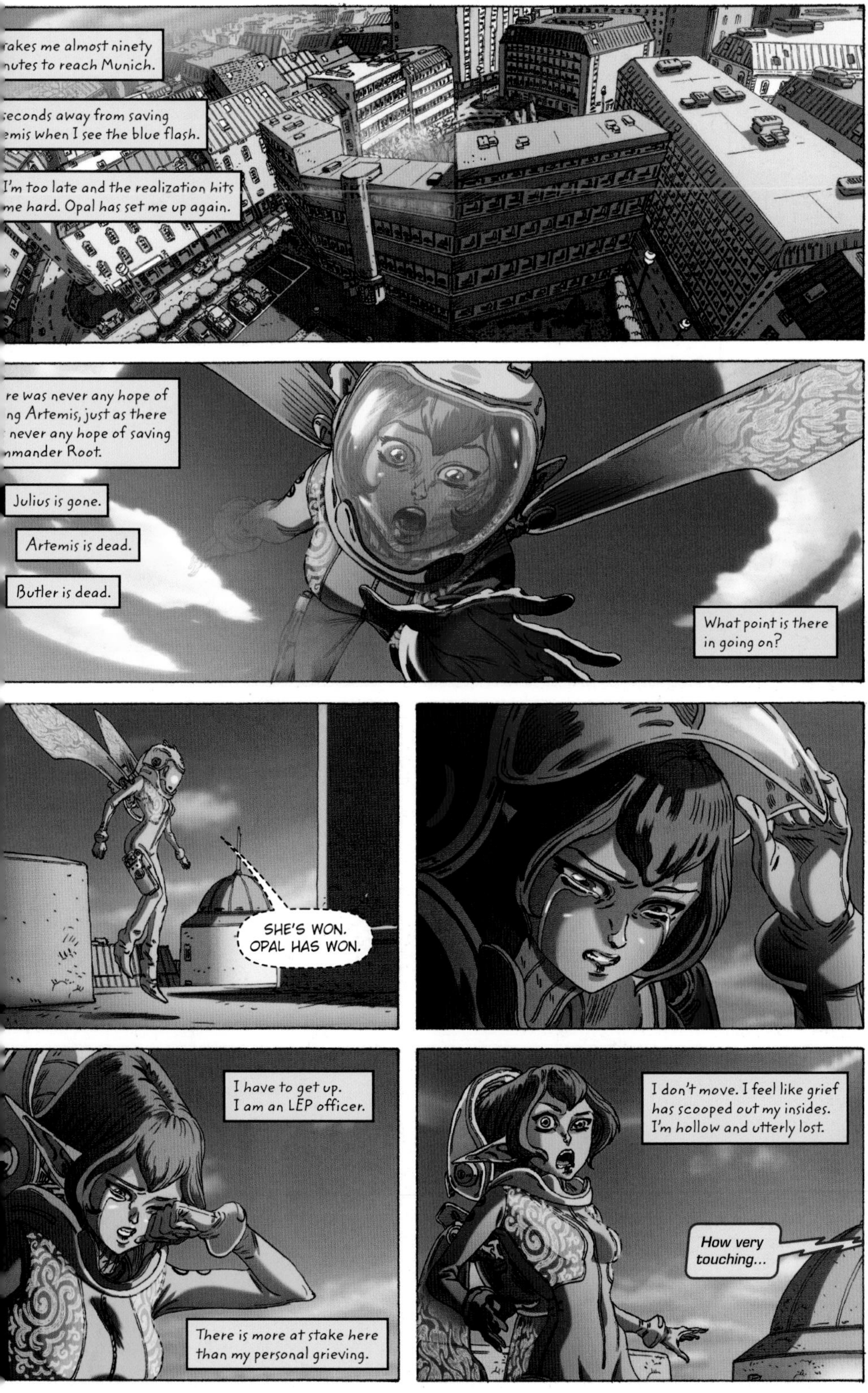
akes me almost ninety
nutes to reach Munich.
seconds away from saving
emis when I see the blue flash.
I'm too late and the realization hits
me hard. Opal has set me up again.
re was never any hope of
ng Artemis, just as there
never any hope of saving
nmander Root.
Julius is gone.
Artemis is dead.
Butler is dead.
What point is there
in going on?
SHE'S WON.
OPAL HAS WON.
I have to get up.
I am an LEP officer.
There is more at stake here
than my personal grieving.
I don't move. I feel like grief
has scooped out my insides.
I'm hollow and utterly lost.
How very
touching...

KOBOI. COME TO GLOAT?

Actually, yes. I followed you from the chute because I wanted to see what total despair looks like.

It's not very fetching, is it?

DETONATE AND GET IT OVER WITH.

Oh, I will. But it's what happens after that's important.

DON'T TELL ME, KOBOI: WORLD DOMINATION.

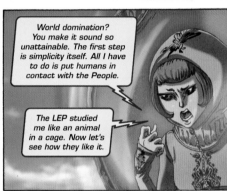

World domination? You make it sound so unattainable. The first step is simplicity itself. All I have to do is put humans in contact with the People.

The LEP studied me like an animal in a cage. Now let's see how they like it.

ALL THIS FOR A CHILDISH PIXIE'S REVENGE?

Oh I'm not a pixie anymore. Look...no pointy ears. I intend to be on the winning side once that probe goes down.

WHAT PROBE?

Enough explaining. You cost me a year of my life, Short. A year.

On the screen I s the hatred in Op eyes. Then she h up a small remot presses the butto

I have seconds before the bio-bomb explodes.

The killing agent in a bio-bomb is solinium, and LEP helmets are supposed to be able to deflect solinium flares.

Let's see if they can.

I hook my helmet ove the bomb point it aw from me.

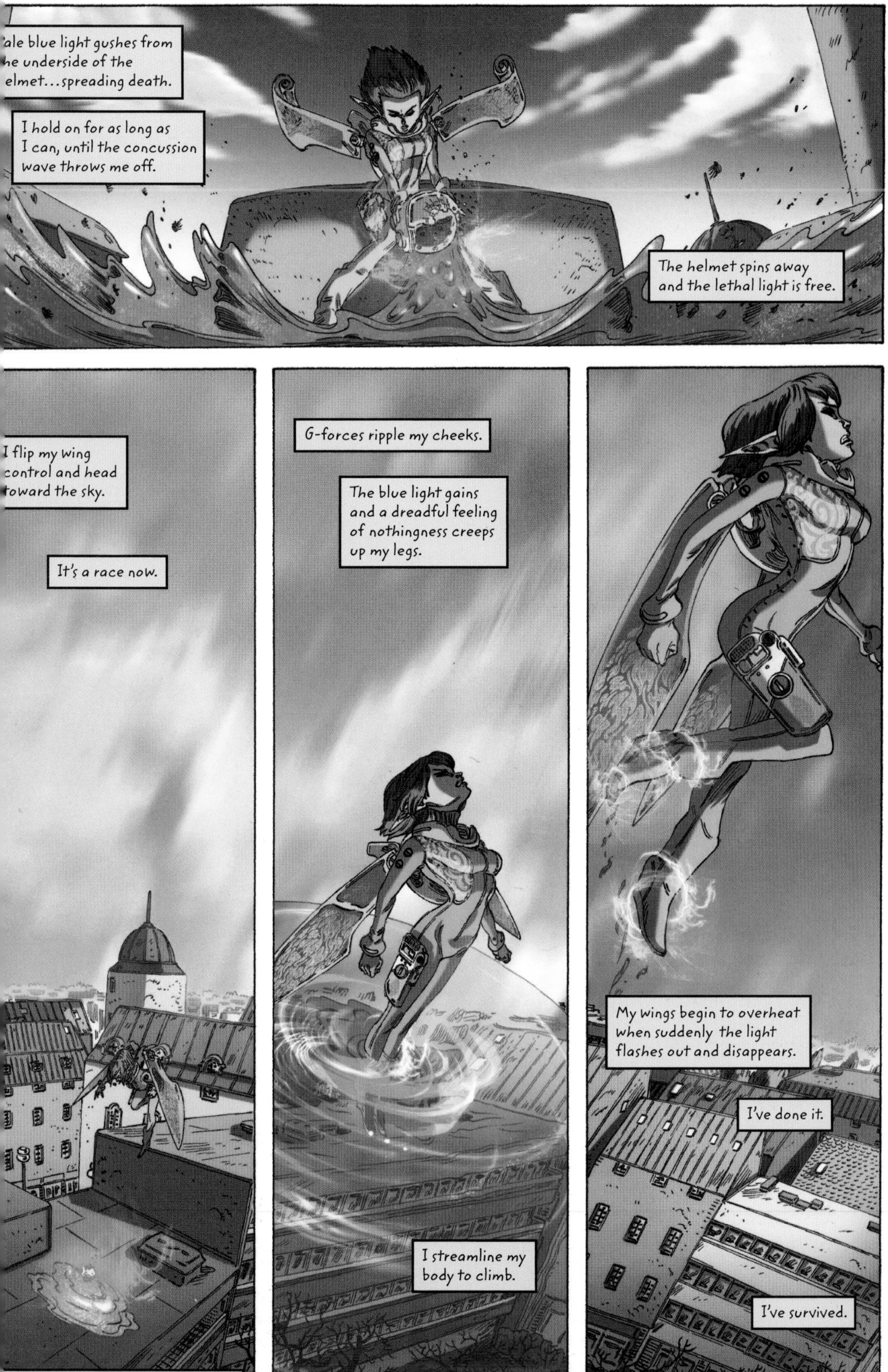
ale blue light gushes from he underside of the elmet...spreading death.
I hold on for as long as I can, until the concussion wave throws me off.
The helmet spins away and the lethal light is free.
I flip my wing control and head toward the sky.
It's a race now.
The bio-bomb blast rises like a wall of death and I have to outrun it.
G-forces ripple my cheeks.
The blue light gains and a dreadful feeling of nothingness creeps up my legs.
I streamline my body to climb.
My wings begin to overheat when suddenly the light flashes out and disappears.
I've done it.
I've survived.

Magic begins to heal my legs.

Next I have to get back underground and warn the LEP about Opal.

My burned-out helmet is the only sign that I was ever on the hotel roof.

When the helmet shorted out so did all of my bio-readings.

As far as the LEP and Opal are concerned I am now officially dead. And being dead might have possibili

Something catches my eye.

Below me, the roof of a hut has caved in. Two figures are lying in the remains.

Please. Please.

It's them.

Both breathing.

There's blood everywhere and Artemis is going into shock. I have to be fast.

I heal them both.

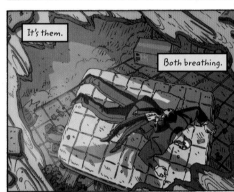

Butler is simply too bulky to move.

GOOD-BYE, OLD FRIEND. I'LL BE BACK FOR YOU.

I hate to leave but I have to ge Artemis to safe

If Opal insists on joining the world of men, then Artemis is surely the ideal foil for her genius.

I shield Artemis as best I can and open the throttle on my wings.

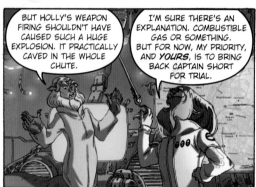

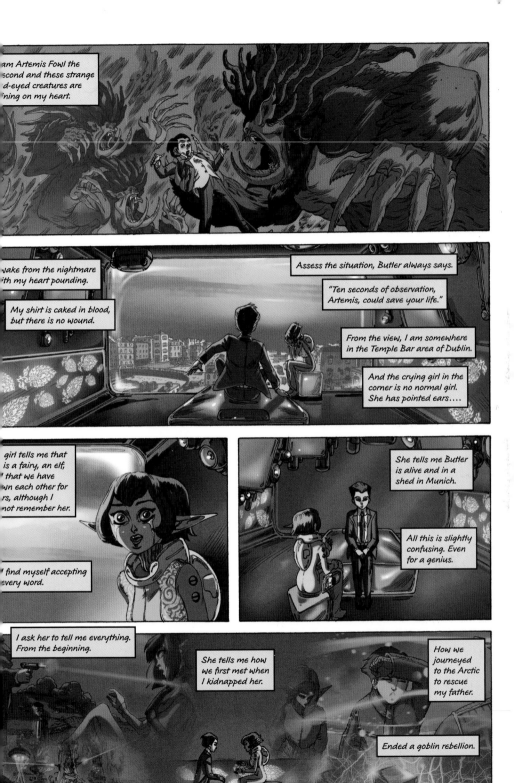

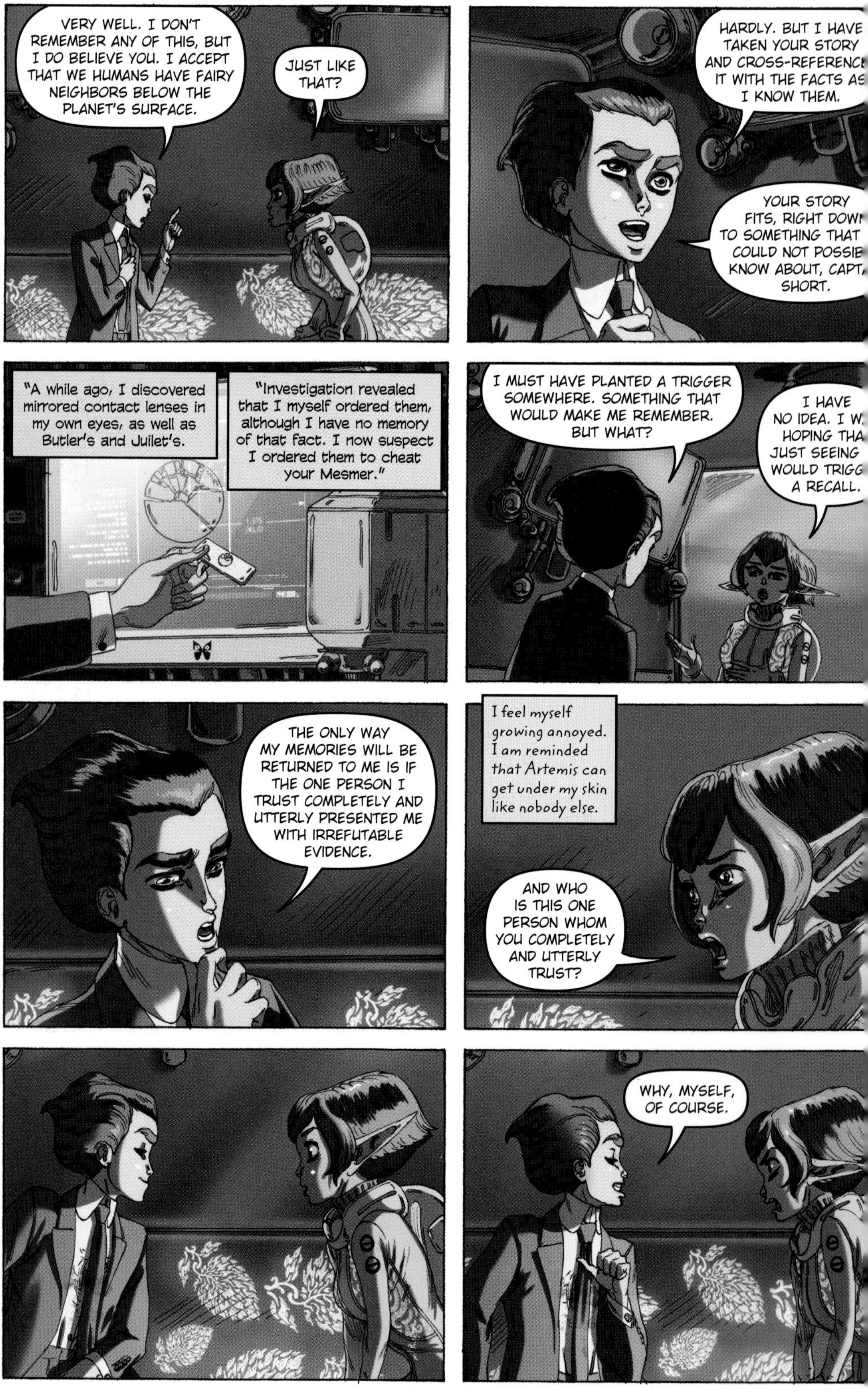

VERY WELL. I DON'T REMEMBER ANY OF THIS, BUT I DO BELIEVE YOU. I ACCEPT THAT WE HUMANS HAVE FAIRY NEIGHBORS BELOW THE PLANET'S SURFACE.
JUST LIKE THAT?
HARDLY. BUT I HAVE TAKEN YOUR STORY AND CROSS-REFERENC IT WITH THE FACTS AS I KNOW THEM.
YOUR STORY FITS, RIGHT DOW TO SOMETHING THAT COULD NOT POSSIB KNOW ABOUT, CAPT SHORT.
"A while ago, I discovered mirrored contact lenses in my own eyes, as well as Butler's and Juilet's.
"Investigation revealed that I myself ordered them, although I have no memory of that fact. I now suspect I ordered them to cheat your Mesmer."
I MUST HAVE PLANTED A TRIGGER SOMEWHERE. SOMETHING THAT WOULD MAKE ME REMEMBER. BUT WHAT?
I HAVE NO IDEA. I W HOPING THA JUST SEEING WOULD TRIGG A RECALL.
THE ONLY WAY MY MEMORIES WILL BE RETURNED TO ME IS IF THE ONE PERSON I TRUST COMPLETELY AND UTTERLY PRESENTED ME WITH IRREFUTABLE EVIDENCE.
I feel myself growing annoyed. I am reminded that Artemis can get under my skin like nobody else.
AND WHO IS THIS ONE PERSON WHOM YOU COMPLETELY AND UTTERLY TRUST?
WHY, MYSELF, OF COURSE.

NICH.

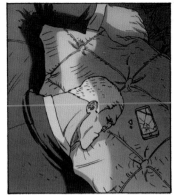

EXCUSE ME, ARE YOU ALIVE?

I AM ALIVE. WHERE IS THE BOY WHO WAS WITH ME?

BOY? THERE IS NO BOY.

OF COURSE, THERE WAS NO BOY.

FORGIVE ME; THE MIND TENDS TO WANDER AFTER A THREE-STORY FALL.

"Artemis, I'm assuming you are ...e and I am leaving this message ... your mobile phone. If you've been ...apped the kidnappers will contact ...owl Manor with their demands."

"If you've simply removed yourself from danger then you will head for home."

"Either way, the trail leads to Fowl Manor and that's where I'm heading now."

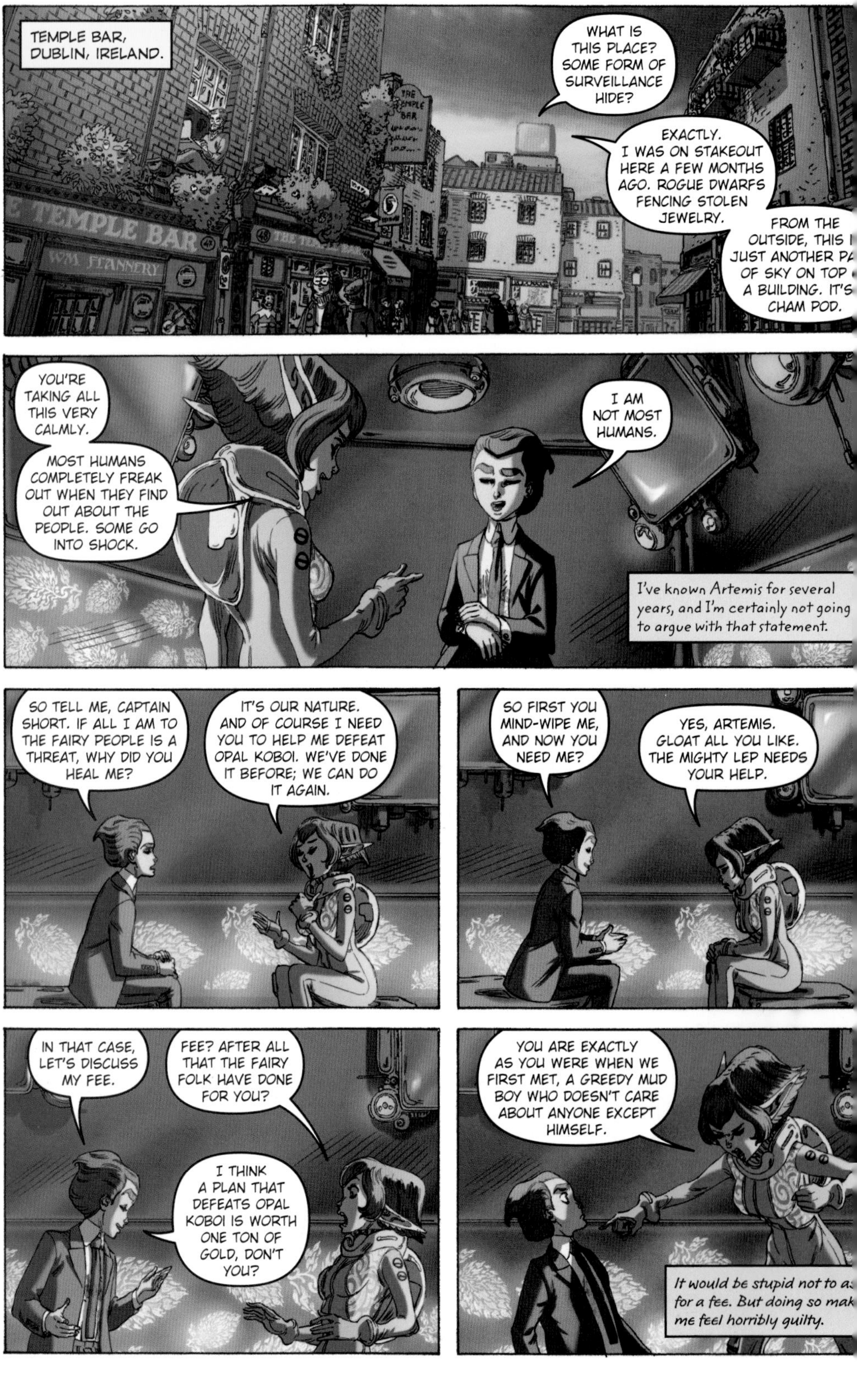
TEMPLE BAR, DUBLIN, IRELAND.
WHAT IS THIS PLACE? SOME FORM OF SURVEILLANCE HIDE?
EXACTLY. I WAS ON STAKEOUT HERE A FEW MONTHS AGO. ROGUE DWARFS FENCING STOLEN JEWELRY.
FROM THE OUTSIDE, THIS I JUST ANOTHER PA OF SKY ON TOP A BUILDING. IT'S CHAM POD.
YOU'RE TAKING ALL THIS VERY CALMLY.
MOST HUMANS COMPLETELY FREAK OUT WHEN THEY FIND OUT ABOUT THE PEOPLE. SOME GO INTO SHOCK.
I AM NOT MOST HUMANS.
I've known Artemis for several years, and I'm certainly not going to argue with that statement.
SO TELL ME, CAPTAIN SHORT. IF ALL I AM TO THE FAIRY PEOPLE IS A THREAT, WHY DID YOU HEAL ME?
IT'S OUR NATURE. AND OF COURSE I NEED YOU TO HELP ME DEFEAT OPAL KOBOI. WE'VE DONE IT BEFORE; WE CAN DO IT AGAIN.
SO FIRST YOU MIND-WIPE ME, AND NOW YOU NEED ME?
YES, ARTEMIS. GLOAT ALL YOU LIKE. THE MIGHTY LEP NEEDS YOUR HELP.
IN THAT CASE, LET'S DISCUSS MY FEE.
FEE? AFTER ALL THAT THE FAIRY FOLK HAVE DONE FOR YOU?
I THINK A PLAN THAT DEFEATS OPAL KOBOI IS WORTH ONE TON OF GOLD, DON'T YOU?
YOU ARE EXACTLY AS YOU WERE WHEN WE FIRST MET, A GREEDY MUD BOY WHO DOESN'T CARE ABOUT ANYONE EXCEPT HIMSELF.
It would be stupid not to as for a fee. But doing so mak me feel horribly guilty.

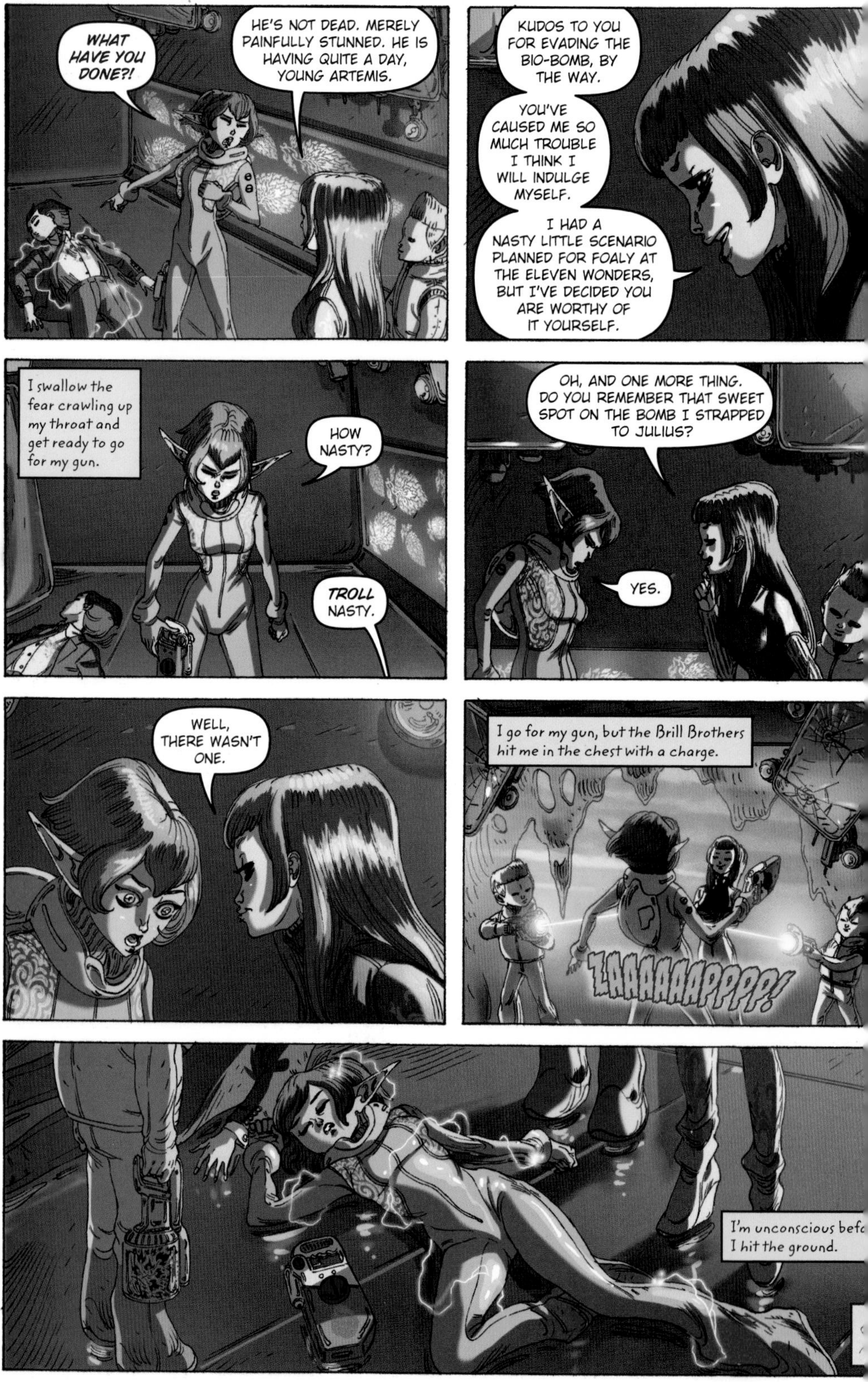
WHAT HAVE YOU DONE?!
HE'S NOT DEAD. MERELY PAINFULLY STUNNED. HE IS HAVING QUITE A DAY, YOUNG ARTEMIS.
KUDOS TO YOU FOR EVADING THE BIO-BOMB, BY THE WAY.
YOU'VE CAUSED ME SO MUCH TROUBLE I THINK I WILL INDULGE MYSELF.
I HAD A NASTY LITTLE SCENARIO PLANNED FOR FOALY AT THE ELEVEN WONDERS, BUT I'VE DECIDED YOU ARE WORTHY OF IT YOURSELF.
I swallow the fear crawling up my throat and get ready to go for my gun.
HOW NASTY?
TROLL NASTY.
OH, AND ONE MORE THING. DO YOU REMEMBER THAT SWEET SPOT ON THE BOMB I STRAPPED TO JULIUS?
YES.
WELL, THERE WASN'T ONE.
I go for my gun, but the Brill Brothers hit me in the chest with a charge.
ZAAAAAAPPPP!
I'm unconscious befo
I hit the ground.

FIVE HOURS AGO.

SO YOU KNOW WHAT THIS MASTER THIEF HERE ACTUALLY DID?

GO ON, TELL ME.

CHAPTER 6:
TROLL NASTY

OKAY, FIRST HE STEALS THE JULES RIMET TROPHY FROM THE HUMANS, THEN HE TRIES TO SELL IT TO AN UNDERCOVER LEP FAIRY.

NEXT HE LIFTS SOME OF THE ARTEMIS FOWL GOLD. HE GETS CLEAN AWAY AND LIES LOW IN LOS ANGELES. BUT DO YOU KNOW *HOW* HE LIES LOW?

HE BUYS HIMSELF A PENTHOUSE APARTMENT AND STARTS STEALING ACADEMY AWARDS. NATURALLY, HE GETS HIMSELF CAUGHT AGAIN.

HA HA HA! WHAT A BRAIN! HOW DOES IT FIT INSIDE HIS ITTY-BITTY HEAD?

SHUTTLE
-24-08
NSPORTING
RF FELON
64 — MULCH
GUMS.

LAUGH ALL YOU LIKE, FISHBOY. BY TONIGHT, I'LL BE FREE AND EATING ONE OF YOUR COUSINS FOR DINNER.

OH, YEAH, MULCH, WHAT WILL YOU DO WHEN YOUR APPEAL IS TURNED DOWN? YOU GONNA CRACK UP LIKE A LITTLE GIRL OR TAKE IT REAL STOIC?

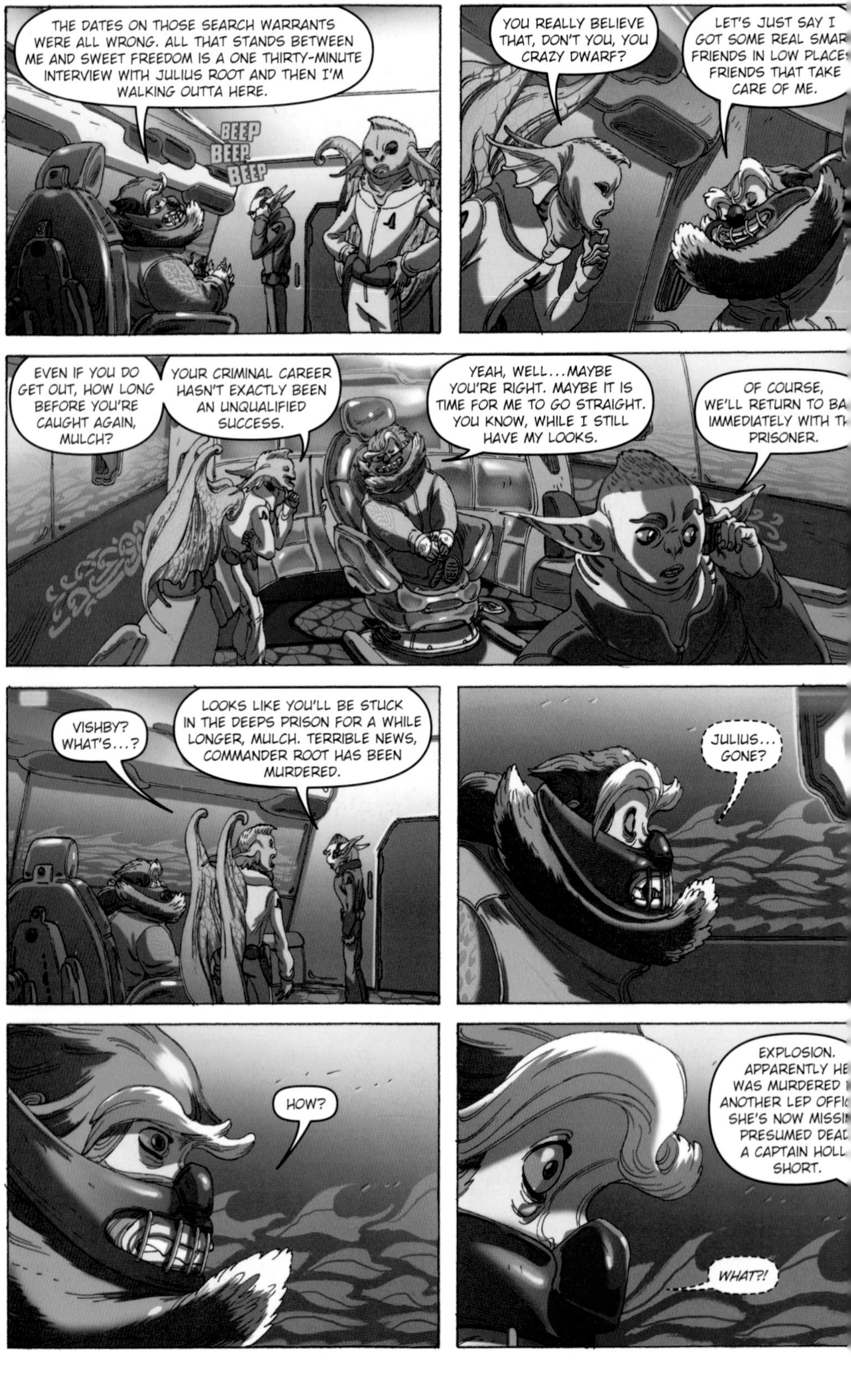
THE DATES ON THOSE SEARCH WARRANTS WERE ALL WRONG. ALL THAT STANDS BETWEEN ME AND SWEET FREEDOM IS A ONE THIRTY-MINUTE INTERVIEW WITH JULIUS ROOT AND THEN I'M WALKING OUTTA HERE.
BEEP
BEEP
BEEP
YOU REALLY BELIEVE THAT, DON'T YOU, YOU CRAZY DWARF?
LET'S JUST SAY I GOT SOME REAL SMAR FRIENDS IN LOW PLACE FRIENDS THAT TAKE CARE OF ME.
EVEN IF YOU DO GET OUT, HOW LONG BEFORE YOU'RE CAUGHT AGAIN, MULCH?
YOUR CRIMINAL CAREER HASN'T EXACTLY BEEN AN UNQUALIFIED SUCCESS.
YEAH, WELL...MAYBE YOU'RE RIGHT. MAYBE IT IS TIME FOR ME TO GO STRAIGHT. YOU KNOW, WHILE I STILL HAVE MY LOOKS.
OF COURSE, WE'LL RETURN TO BA IMMEDIATELY WITH TH PRISONER.
VISHBY? WHAT'S...?
LOOKS LIKE YOU'LL BE STUCK IN THE DEEPS PRISON FOR A WHILE LONGER, MULCH. TERRIBLE NEWS, COMMANDER ROOT HAS BEEN MURDERED.
JULIUS... GONE?
HOW?
EXPLOSION. APPARENTLY HE WAS MURDERED ANOTHER LEP OFFI SHE'S NOW MISSI PRESUMED DEA A CAPTAIN HOLL SHORT.
WHAT?!

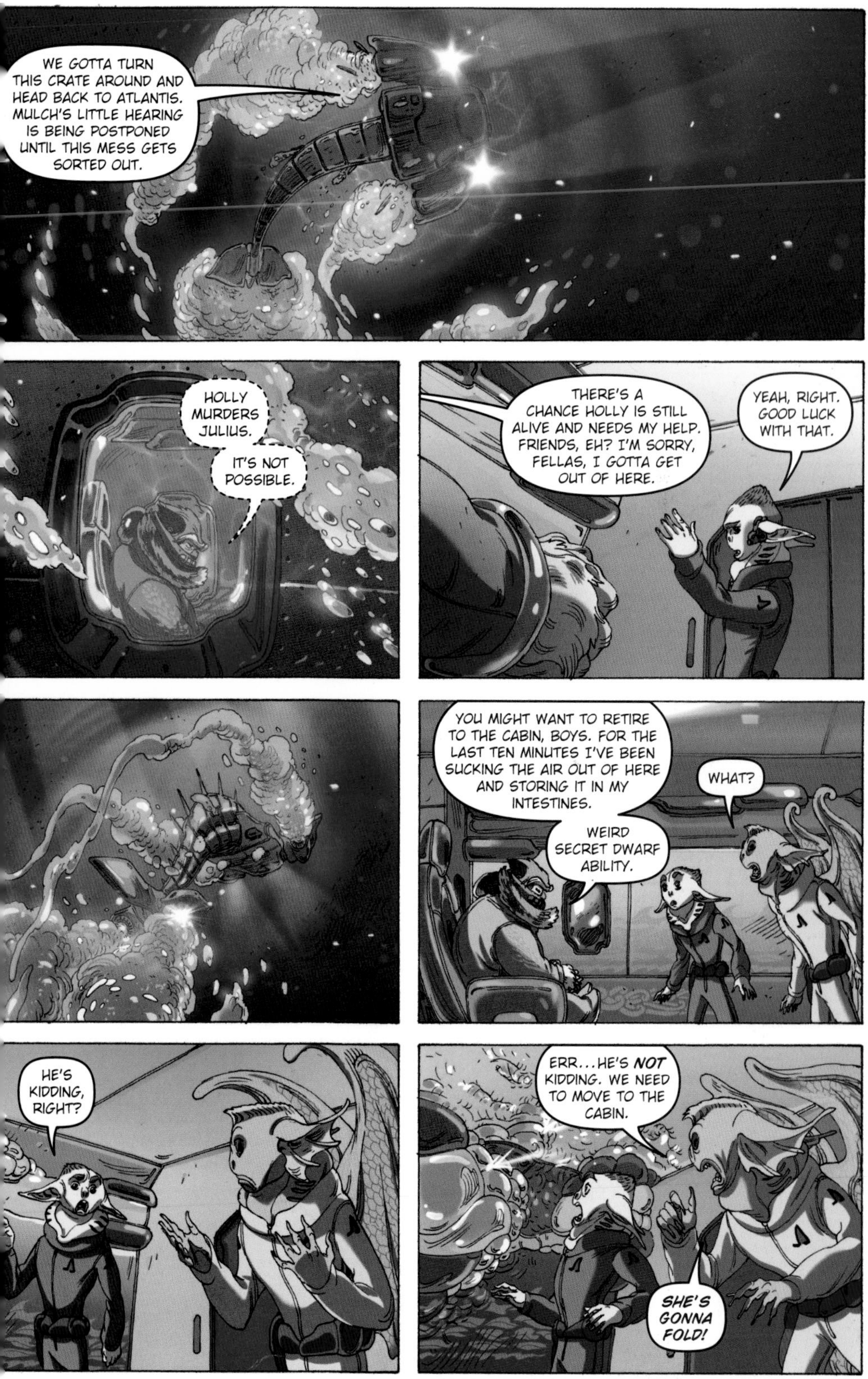
WE GOTTA TURN THIS CRATE AROUND AND HEAD BACK TO ATLANTIS. MULCH'S LITTLE HEARING IS BEING POSTPONED UNTIL THIS MESS GETS SORTED OUT.
HOLLY MURDERS JULIUS.
IT'S NOT POSSIBLE.
THERE'S A CHANCE HOLLY IS STILL ALIVE AND NEEDS MY HELP. FRIENDS, EH? I'M SORRY, FELLAS, I GOTTA GET OUT OF HERE.
YEAH, RIGHT. GOOD LUCK WITH THAT.
YOU MIGHT WANT TO RETIRE TO THE CABIN, BOYS. FOR THE LAST TEN MINUTES I'VE BEEN SUCKING THE AIR OUT OF HERE AND STORING IT IN MY INTESTINES.
WEIRD SECRET DWARF ABILITY.
WHAT?
HE'S KIDDING, RIGHT?
ERR...HE'S *NOT* KIDDING. WE NEED TO MOVE TO THE CABIN.
SHE'S GONNA FOLD!

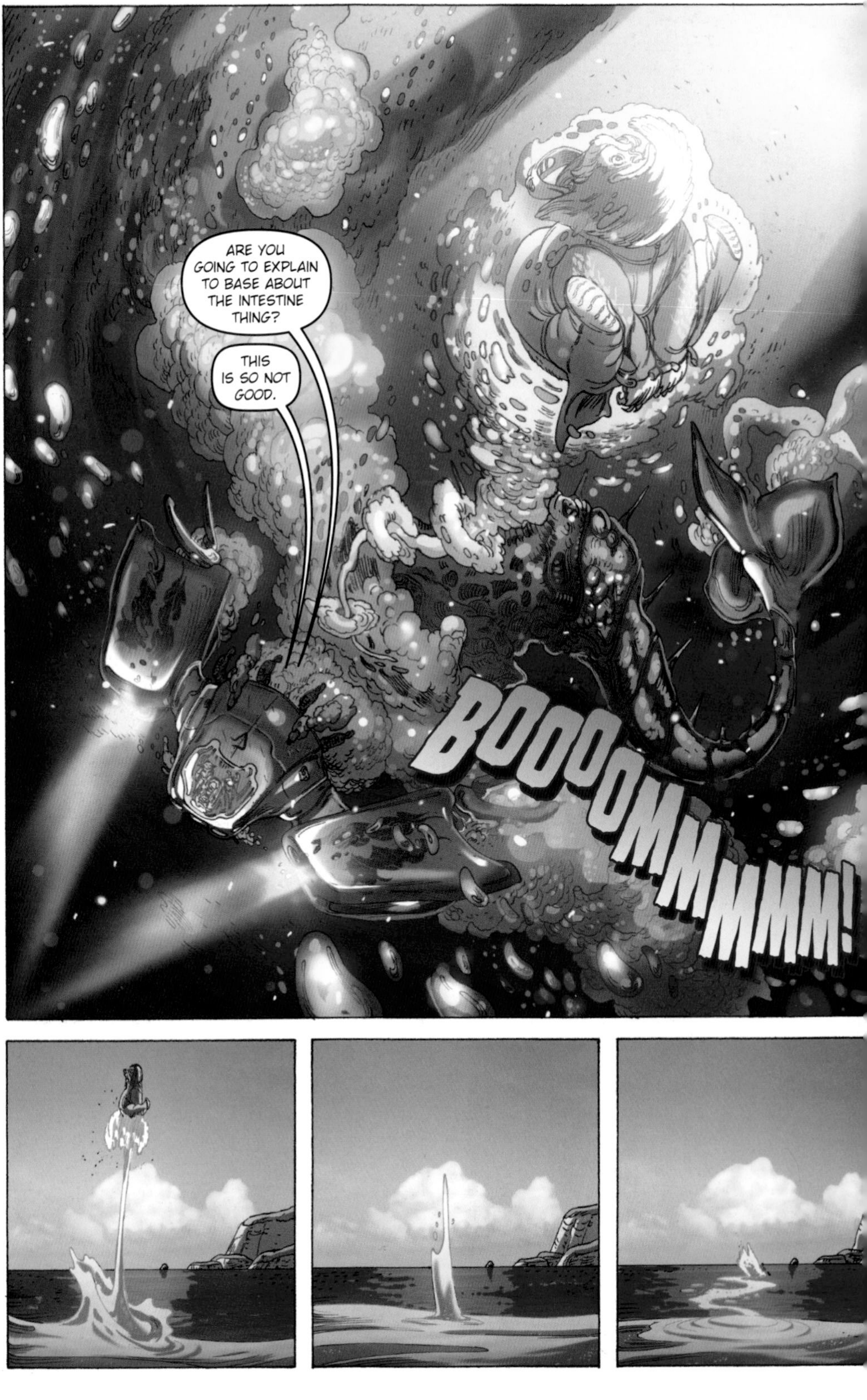
ARE YOU GOING TO EXPLAIN TO BASE ABOUT THE INTESTINE THING?
THIS IS SO NOT GOOD.
BOOOOMMMMMM!

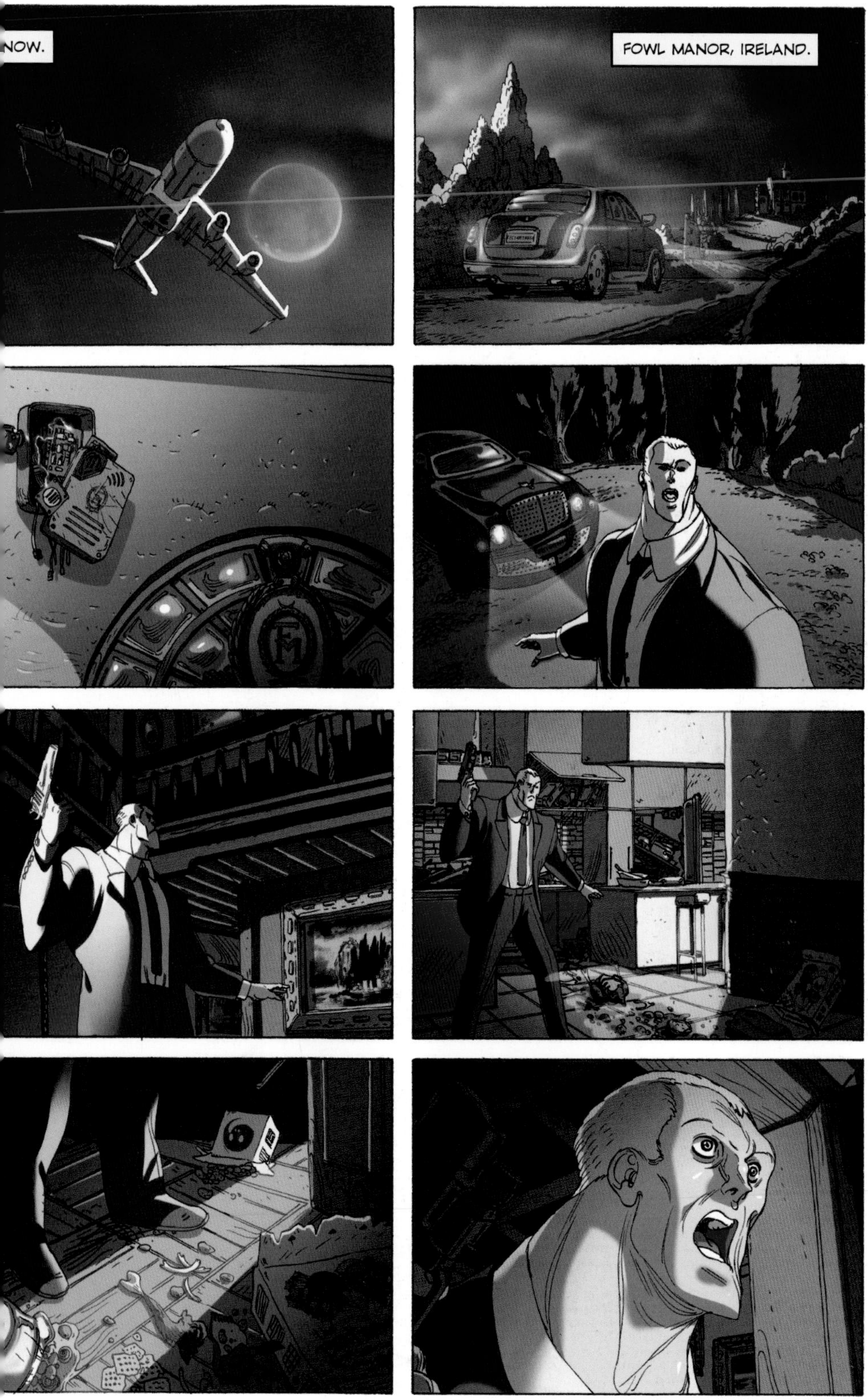
NOW.
FOWL MANOR, IRELAND.

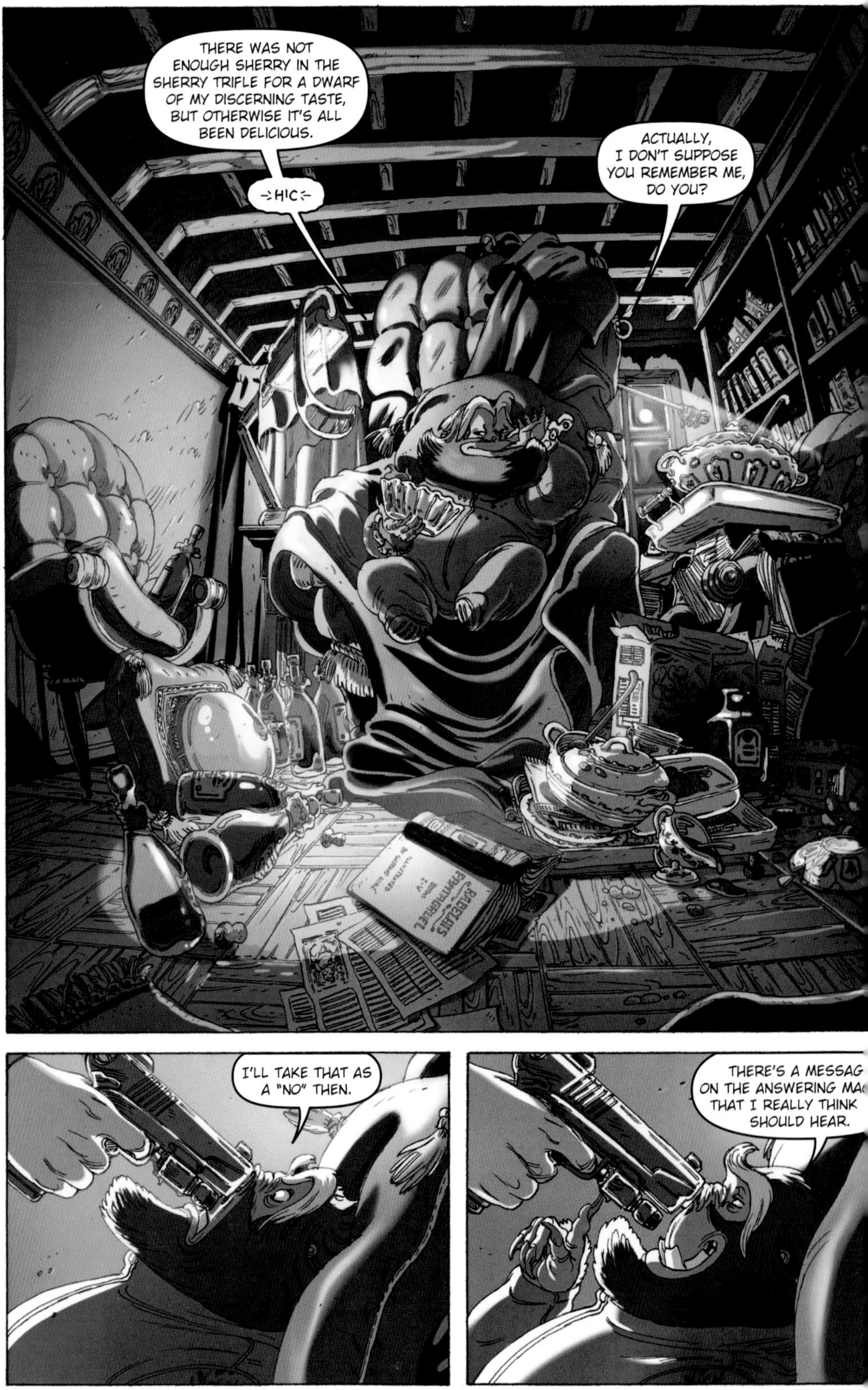
THERE WAS NOT ENOUGH SHERRY IN THE SHERRY TRIFLE FOR A DWARF OF MY DISCERNING TASTE, BUT OTHERWISE IT'S ALL BEEN DELICIOUS.
HIC
ACTUALLY, I DON'T SUPPOSE YOU REMEMBER ME, DO YOU?
I'LL TAKE THAT AS A "NO" THEN.
THERE'S A MESSAG
ON THE ANSWERING MA
THAT I REALLY THINK
SHOULD HEAR.

...at the Eleven Wonders, but I've decided you are worthy of it yourself...

THAT FIRST [H]ALF IS A MESSAGE FROM [AR]TEMIS; THEN IT SOUNDS [LI]KE OPAL CAPTURED HIM AND HOLLY.

BUT HEY, [AT L]EAST THAT MEANS [HOL]LY'S ALIVE, RIGHT?

ELVES?

MAYBE THIS WILL OPEN YOUR MIND? WHEN ARTEMIS GAVE IT TO ME IT WAS PAINTED TO LOOK LIKE A GOLD COIN.

I HANDLED IT SO MUCH THAT SOME OF THE GOLD FLAKED OFF AND I SAW WHAT IT REALLY WAS.

A COMPUTER DISK. IT HAS TO BE A MESSAGE.

ELVES?

COME ON, BIG GUY. JUST PLAY THE DISK.

Hello, Butler. If you are watching this then our [d]ear friend Mister Diggums has come through. [T]here is also a strong possibility that you are [w]atching this at a time of peril, so I'll be brief.

Fairies are real and some of them are our friends.

In order to verify the fantastic facts I am about to reveal, I will say one word. Just one. A word that bodyguard etiquette forbids me to know...unless you told me as you were dying.

Your name, old friend, is Domovoi.

IT'S TRUE. IT'S ALL TRUE. I REMEMBER EVERYTHING.

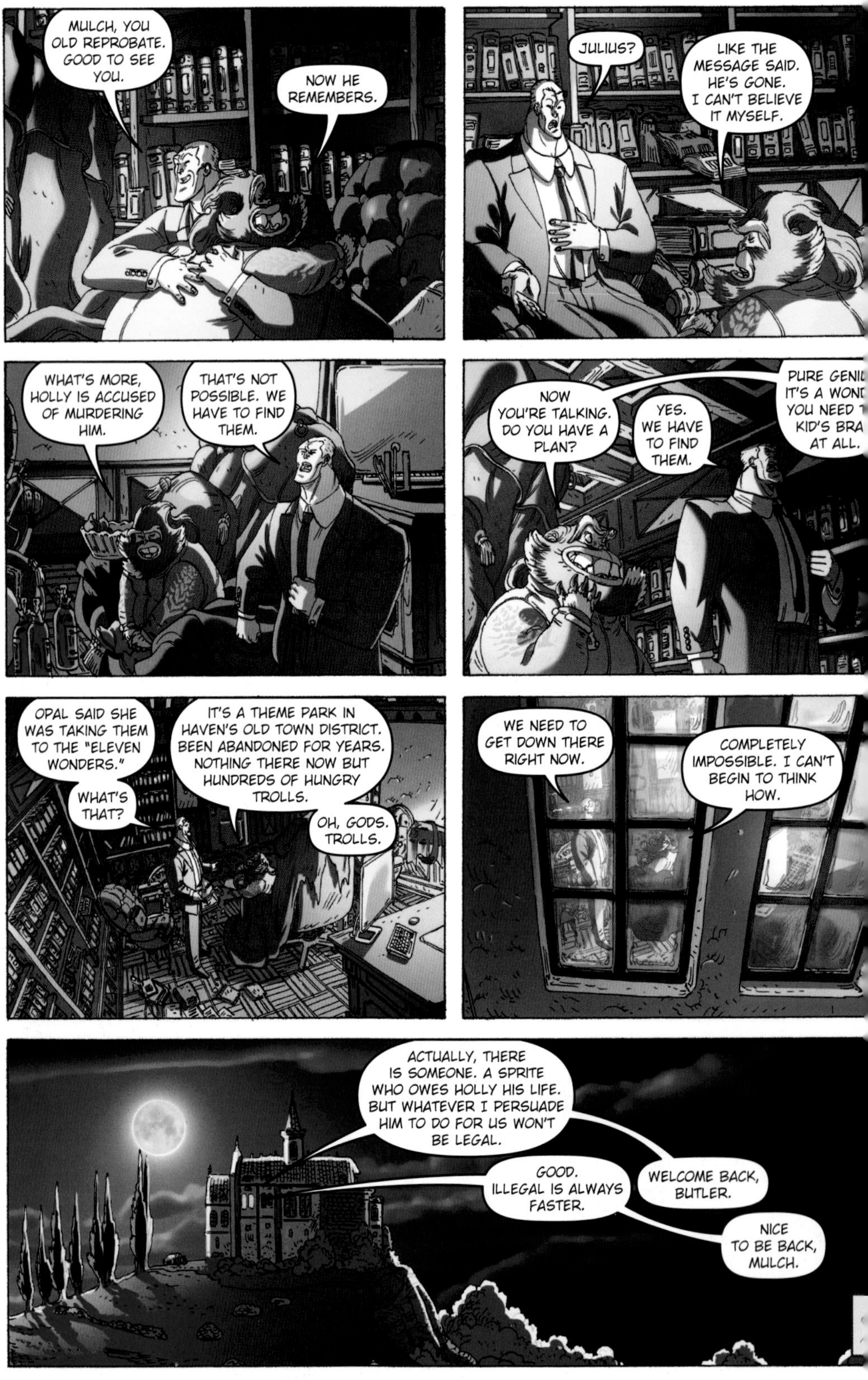
MULCH, YOU OLD REPROBATE. GOOD TO SEE YOU.
NOW HE REMEMBERS.
JULIUS?
LIKE THE MESSAGE SAID. HE'S GONE. I CAN'T BELIEVE IT MYSELF.
WHAT'S MORE, HOLLY IS ACCUSED OF MURDERING HIM.
THAT'S NOT POSSIBLE. WE HAVE TO FIND THEM.
NOW YOU'RE TALKING. DO YOU HAVE A PLAN?
YES. WE HAVE TO FIND THEM.
PURE GENI
IT'S A WON
YOU NEED
KID'S BRA
AT ALL.
OPAL SAID SHE WAS TAKING THEM TO THE "ELEVEN WONDERS."
WHAT'S THAT?
IT'S A THEME PARK IN HAVEN'S OLD TOWN DISTRICT. BEEN ABANDONED FOR YEARS. NOTHING THERE NOW BUT HUNDREDS OF HUNGRY TROLLS.
OH, GODS. TROLLS.
WE NEED TO GET DOWN THERE RIGHT NOW.
COMPLETELY IMPOSSIBLE. I CAN'T BEGIN TO THINK HOW.
ACTUALLY, THERE IS SOMEONE. A SPRITE WHO OWES HOLLY HIS LIFE. BUT WHATEVER I PERSUADE HIM TO DO FOR US WON'T BE LEGAL.
WELCOME BACK, BUTLER.
GOOD. ILLEGAL IS ALWAYS FASTER.
NICE TO BE BACK, MULCH.

LOWER ELEMENTS.

KOBOI'S SHUTTLE—
CEPT MODEL THAT
WENT INTO MASS
UCTION. ITS OUTER
S STEALTH ORE AND
OIL.

ST—
SOLUTELY
RBITANT.

SECURE THE PRISONERS IN THE PASSENGER BAY AND GET ME A FACE LINK TO GIOVANNI ZITO IN SICILY.

AT ONCE, MISTRESS.

CHAPTER 7: THE TEMPLE OF ARTEMIS

Belinda, my ar daughter. s that you? hen are you ming home?

YES, PAPA. IT'S ME. HOW IS EVERYTHING THERE?

Molto bene. Wonderful. The mountains are beautiful. The skiing is...

IDIOTA...

HOW IS EVERYTHING WITH THE PROBE? ARE WE ON SCHEDULE?

Yes, my dear. Everything is n schedule. The explosive ds are being buried today. e probe's systems check as a resounding success. We are on course.

EXCELLENT, PAPA. YOU ARE SO GOOD TO YOUR LITTLE BELINDA. I WILL BE WITH YOU SOON.

Hurry home, my dear.

HOW LONG TO THE THEME PARK?

WE'VE ENTERED THE MAIN CHUTE NETWORK. FIVE HOURS. MAYBE LESS.

TO GIVE HOLLY AND ARTEMIS WHAT THEY DESERVE, I THINK I CAN SPARE *FIVE* HOURS.

The Brill Brothers help us back into consciousness with a buzz baton.

OUCH!

WELCOME BACK TO THE LAND OF THE CONDEMNED. HOW DO YOU LIKE MY SHUTTLE?

OUCH!

UH! THESE SEATS ARE REAL FUR! YOU ARE DISGUSTING, KOBOI.

SKINNING ANIMALS FOR FASHION IS WH[...] HUMANS DO AND I'M HUM[...] NOW.

I KNOW THEY MIND-WIPED YOU, ARTEMIS. BUT SURELY YOU HAVE YOUR MEMORIES BACK BY NOW?

ACTUALLY, I DON'T. BUT I'VE HEARD HOW FOALY DEFEATED YOU WITH SUPERIOR INTELLECT. I'M CERTAIN HE WILL DO IT AGAIN.

THAT RIDICULOUS CENTAUR! HE WAS LUCKY AND I WAS HAMPERED BY THAT IDIOT, CUDGEON. NOT THIS TIME.

THIS TIME I AM THE ARCHITECT OF MY OWN FATE. AND OF *YOURS.*

I HAVE A GRANDER VISION. I WILL LEAD THE HUMANS TO THE PEOPLE. WHEN THE TWO WORLDS COLLIDE, THERE WILL BE A WAR AND MY ADOPTED PEOPLE WILL WIN. I'LL MAKE SURE OF THAT.

MADAM, WE'RE NEARLY HERE.

THE ELEVEN WONDERS THEME PARK IN HAVEN'S OLD TOWN DISTRICT.

BRAINCHILD OF A BILLIONAIRE PIXIE WHO WANTED TO CASH IN ON THE PEOPLE'S FASCINATION WITH MUD MEN.

THE PARK WAS BUILT ON CHEAP REAL ESTATE. THE TUNNELS HERE WERE DECLARED UNSAFE LONG AGO.

TEN THOUSAND YEARS OF CIVILIZATION AND YOU ONLY MANAGE TO PRODUCE ELEVEN SO-CALLED WONDERS.

YOU KNOW OF COURSE THAT THERE ARE ONLY SEVEN WONDERS ON THE OFFICIAL LIST.

YOU HUMANS ARE SO NARROW-MINDED.

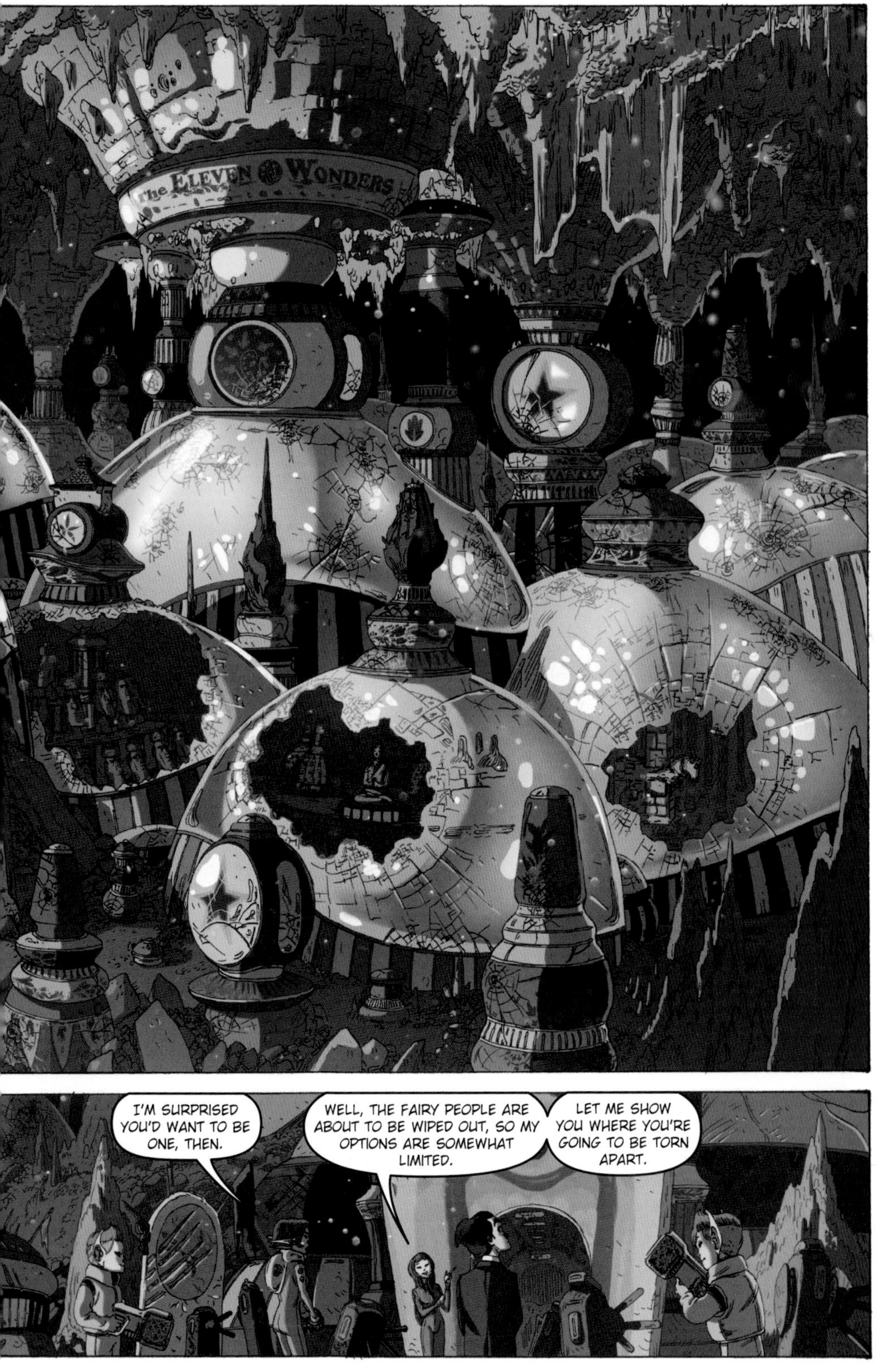
The ELEVEN WONDERS
I'M SURPRISED YOU'D WANT TO BE ONE, THEN.
WELL, THE FAIRY PEOPLE ARE ABOUT TO BE WIPED OUT, SO MY OPTIONS ARE SOMEWHAT LIMITED.
LET ME SHOW YOU WHERE YOU'RE GOING TO BE TORN APART.

NOW I MUST WARN YOU, THE TROLLS ARE EXTREMELY TERRITORIAL. THEY DON'T GET MUCH TO EAT OUT HERE EXCEPT OTHER TROLLS.

CUBS AND STRAGGLERS ARE PICKED OFF BY THE BULLS AND THEN BUTCHERED WITH TEETH, CLAWS, AND TUSKS.

IT'S A[L] RATHE[R] UNPLEAS[ANT] I'M AFR[AID]

HERE WE ARE...THE TEMPLE OF ARTEMIS. NOW, WHY DO YOU SUPPOSE SOMEONE WOULD NAME A MALE CHILD AFTER A FEMALE GODDESS?

IT'S MY FATHER'S NAME. IT CAN BE USED FOR GIRLS OR BOYS. AND IT MEANS "THE HUNTER." RATHER APT, DON'T YOU THINK?

IT MAY INTEREST YOU TO KNOW THAT YOUR CHOSEN HUMAN NAME OF BELINDA MEANS "BEAUTIFUL SNAKE." ALSO RATHER FITTING. HALF OF IT, ANYWAY.

YOU ARE A VERY ANNOYING CREATURE, FOWL.

SPRAY THEM.

ZZZZAW HHHT-TT

TROLL PHEROMONE[S] YOU NOW SM[ELL] LIKE FEMAL[E] TROLLS IN HEAT.

GOOD LUCK WH[EN] THEY FIN[D] OUT YOU'[RE] NOT.

I'VE REMOVED THE WINGS FROM YOUR SUIT BUT I'VE LEFT THE HEATING COILS.

AFTER ALL, EVERYONE DESERVES A SPORTING CHANCE.

A LOT OF USE HEATING COILS WILL BE AGAINST TROLLS.

Opal leaves us. We're alone a[nd] unarmed with a hundred very hungry trolls. Oh, and we sme[ll] like the female of the species.

Holly heads for an artificial river running through the exhibit.

"Okay, Mud Boy. Into the water."

Holly dives into the river, arcing gracefully through the air.

I tumble in after [...] Gulping down wa[...] and close to pani[...]

Agair[...]

The trolls do not follow us into the water. We're safe. For now.

This is an artificial river. It's filter[...] through a central tank.

Sounds like th[...] our way out! I[...] don't drown fi[...]

We float with the current. Our hungry friends keep pace on the bank.

The water carries us, quicker and quicker, toward the whirlpool ahead.

There is only water now.

Water and confusic[...]

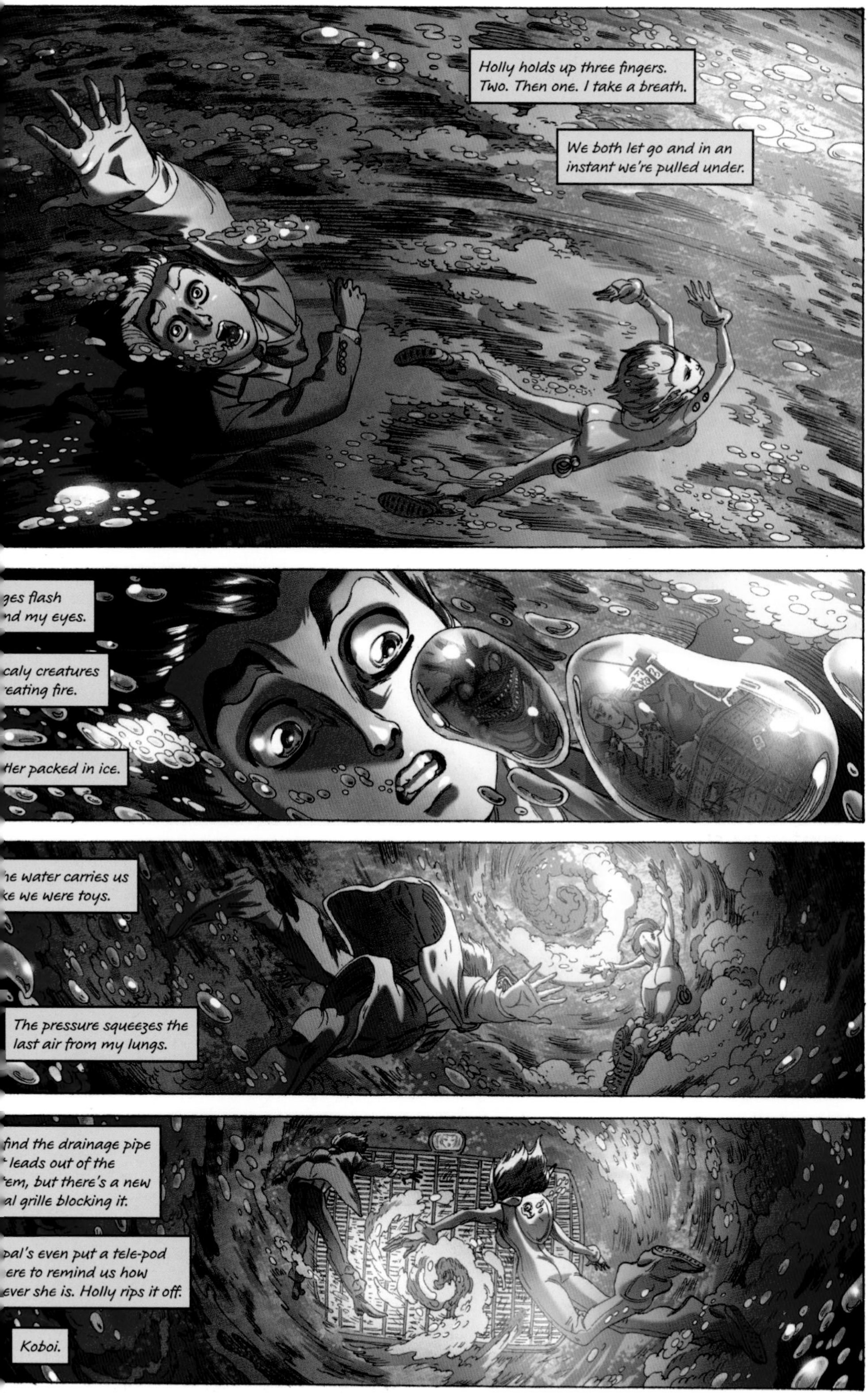
Holly holds up three fingers. Two. Then one. I take a breath.
We both let go and in an instant we're pulled under.
ges flash nd my eyes.
caly creatures eating fire.
packed in ice.
he water carries us ke we were toys.
The pressure squeezes the last air from my lungs.
find the drainage pipe leads out of the em, but there's a new al grille blocking it.
pal's even put a tele-pod ere to remind us how ever she is. Holly rips it off.
Koboi.

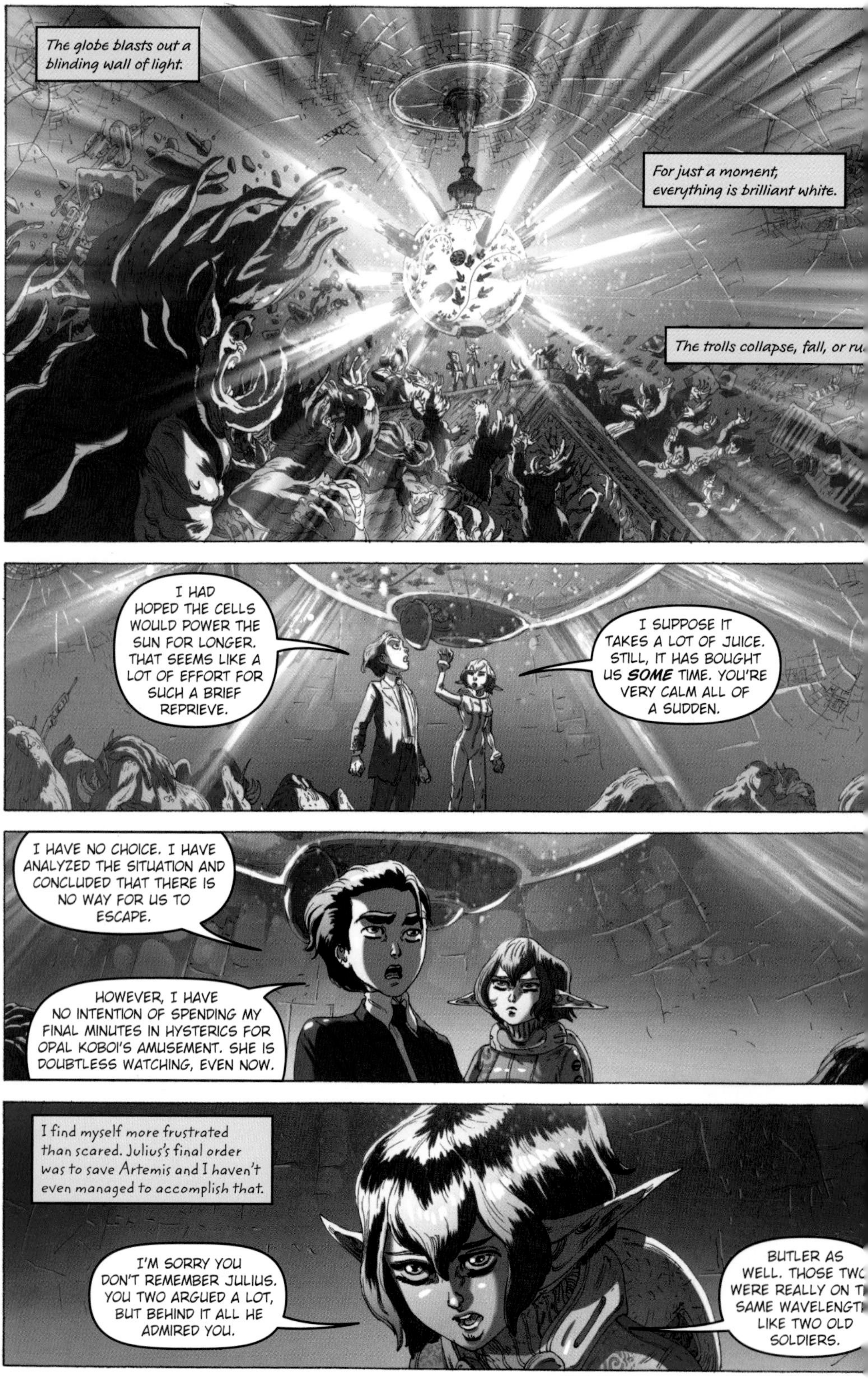
The globe blasts out a blinding wall of light.
For just a moment, everything is brilliant white.
The trolls collapse, fall, or ru
I HAD HOPED THE CELLS WOULD POWER THE SUN FOR LONGER. THAT SEEMS LIKE A LOT OF EFFORT FOR SUCH A BRIEF REPRIEVE.
I SUPPOSE IT TAKES A LOT OF JUICE. STILL, IT HAS BOUGHT US SOME TIME. YOU'RE VERY CALM ALL OF A SUDDEN.
I HAVE NO CHOICE. I HAVE ANALYZED THE SITUATION AND CONCLUDED THAT THERE IS NO WAY FOR US TO ESCAPE.
HOWEVER, I HAVE NO INTENTION OF SPENDING MY FINAL MINUTES IN HYSTERICS FOR OPAL KOBOI'S AMUSEMENT. SHE IS DOUBTLESS WATCHING, EVEN NOW.
I find myself more frustrated than scared. Julius's final order was to save Artemis and I haven't even managed to accomplish that.
I'M SORRY YOU DON'T REMEMBER JULIUS. YOU TWO ARGUED A LOT, BUT BEHIND IT ALL HE ADMIRED YOU.
BUTLER AS WELL. THOSE TWO WERE REALLY ON T SAME WAVELENGT LIKE TWO OLD SOLDIERS.

The creature scampers up the rope and we follow him into a shuttle before the trolls can recover.

BUTLER!

And suddenly in spite of everything, I f[e]el completely sa[fe].

WELL, WE SURVIVED. DOES THAT MEAN WE'RE FRIENDS NOW? BONDED BY TRAUMA?

YES, ALTHOUGH I MAY HAVE TO READ UP ON WHAT HAVING A FRIEND ACTUALLY INVOLVES.

THE THRILL OF SURVIVAL MIGHT BE AFFECTING MY JUDGMENT, BUT...

BUT...?

I DON'T FEEL I SHOULD BE PAID TO HELP A FRIEND. KEEP YOUR FAIRY GOLD.

Holly smiles with genuine warmth for the first time today.

WITH THE FOUR OF US ON HER TRAIL, ARTEMIS, OPAL KOBOI DOESN'T STAND A CHANCE.

Holly's eyes flash with a hint of steel.

I only hope she's right.

CHAPTER 8:

SOME INTELLIGENT CONVERSATION

That's what Father would do.

I find a computer in the rear of the shuttle.

I don't know if this is all real. But if there's a danger of a war between fairies and humans I have to find out.

I take a breath ana then push in the di.

Within seconds, I'm looking at myself on screen.

"How nice for you to see me. Doubtless this will be the first intelligent conversation you have had for some time."

It's a message I recorded to myself before I apparently went to Chicago to deal with a Jon Spiro.

Images flash from the screen, filling in empty spaces in my head.

I had the mirrored contact lenses mac myself to avoid being mesmerized.

I put the wrong date on the search warrants for Mulch.

It's all true.

And suddenly...

I remember everything.

all the memories
things I'm proud of.

I kidnapped Holly
and imprisoned her.

How could I have done that?

I know it all now.

Commander
Root is gone.
She took him
from his People.

I beat Koboi before and I will beat her again.

e is one thought in my head,
persistent than all the rest.

Friends.

ARTEMIS,
ARE YOU...

I'M BACK. I REMEMBER
EVERYTHING.

I have friends.

COMPUTER DISK
VE TO MULCH TO
P SAFE DID THE
TRICK.

BUT THE
ONLY THING YOU
GAVE TO MULCH
WAS THE GOLD
MEDALLION.

EXACTLY.
I AM A GENIUS,
AFTER ALL.

HOLLY, I'M SO SORRY
ABOUT JULIUS. I KNOW OUR
RELATIONSHIP WAS ROCKY,
BUT I HAD NOTHING BUT
RESPECT FOR HIM.

There are tears
in Holly's eyes
and she nods.

NOW WE'RE ALL REACQUAINTED, WE NEED TO LOCATE OPAL KOBOI. SHE COULD BE ANYWHERE.

NO NEED. I KNOW EXACTLY WHERE OUR WOULD-BE WAR STARTER IS. LIKE ALL MEGALOMANIACS, SHE HAS A TENDENCY TO SHOW OFF.

OPAL REVEALED MORE OF HER PLANS THAN SHE KNEW WHEN SHE SAID HER HUMAN NAME WAS BELINDA ZITO.

IF YOU WISHED TO SOMEHOW LEAD THE HUMANS TO THE FAIRY PEOPLE, WHO BETTER TO ADOPT YOU THAN BILLIONAIRE ENVIRONMENTALIST GIOVANNI ZITO?

THERE'S BEEN A MUD MAN NAMED ZITO ALL OVER THE HUMAN NEWS CHANNELS TODAY. DO YOU THINK IT'S THE SAME ONE?

I REALLY HOPE NOT, BUT I'D BET MY LIFE IT IS.

Of course, it is.

We have sent craft into space, and yet we have no idea what is at the center of our own planet. Today we will make history and find out.

Today, for the first time ever, we will send a probe all the way down into the outer core.

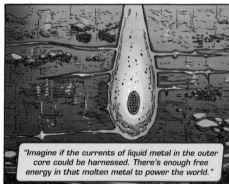

"Imagine if the currents of liquid metal in the outer core could be harnessed. There's enough free energy in that molten metal to power the world."

SO TODAY WE ARE SENDING AN UNMANNED PROBE, BRISTLING WITH SENSORS. WHATEVER IS DOWN THERE, WE WILL FIND IT.

SEVERAL LARGE CHARGES WILL BE DETONATED UNDERGROUND. THEY WILL CREATE A MILLION TONS OF MOLTEN IRON TO ALLOW THE PROBE TO DESCEND.

AND WHEN IS THIS HAPPENING, MR. ZITO?

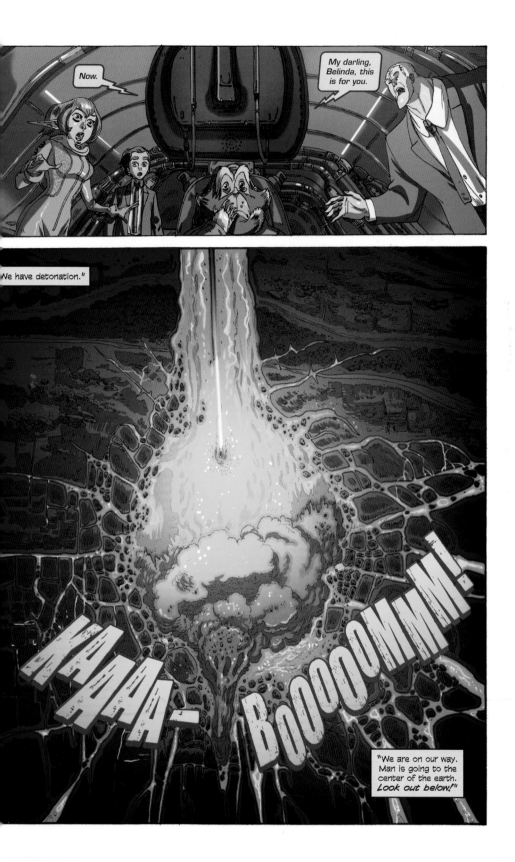

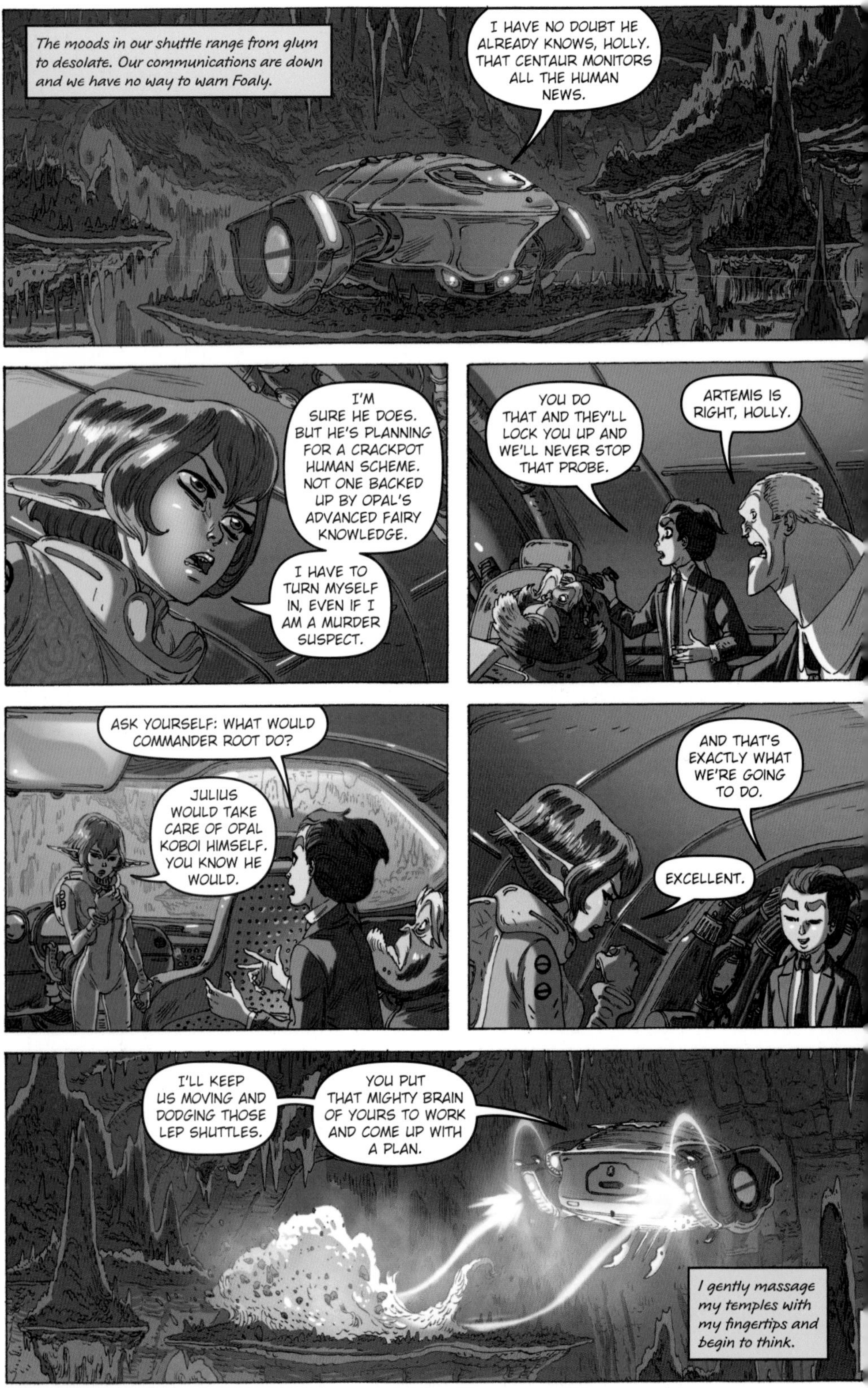

The moods in our shuttle range from glum to desolate. Our communications are down and we have no way to warn Foaly.
I HAVE NO DOUBT HE ALREADY KNOWS, HOLLY. THAT CENTAUR MONITORS ALL THE HUMAN NEWS.
I'M SURE HE DOES. BUT HE'S PLANNING FOR A CRACKPOT HUMAN SCHEME. NOT ONE BACKED UP BY OPAL'S ADVANCED FAIRY KNOWLEDGE.
I HAVE TO TURN MYSELF IN, EVEN IF I AM A MURDER SUSPECT.
YOU DO THAT AND THEY'LL LOCK YOU UP AND WE'LL NEVER STOP THAT PROBE.
ARTEMIS IS RIGHT, HOLLY.
ASK YOURSELF: WHAT WOULD COMMANDER ROOT DO?
JULIUS WOULD TAKE CARE OF OPAL KOBOI HIMSELF. YOU KNOW HE WOULD.
AND THAT'S EXACTLY WHAT WE'RE GOING TO DO.
EXCELLENT.
I'LL KEEP US MOVING AND DODGING THOSE LEP SHUTTLES.
YOU PUT THAT MIGHTY BRAIN OF YOURS TO WORK AND COME UP WITH A PLAN.
I gently massage my temples with my fingertips and begin to think.

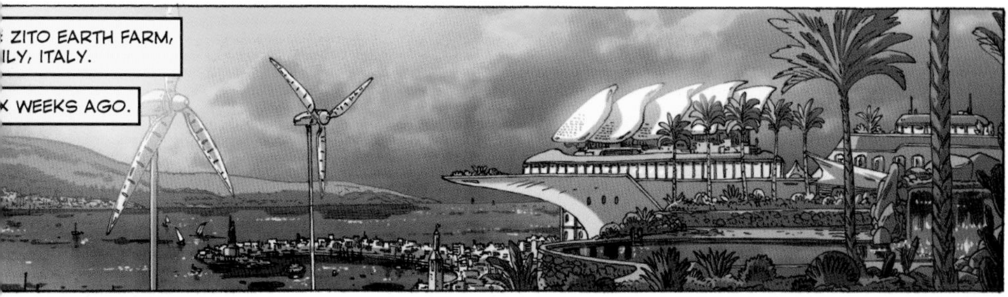

ZITO EARTH FARM,
ILY, ITALY.
K WEEKS AGO.

HAPTER 9: DADDY'S GIRL

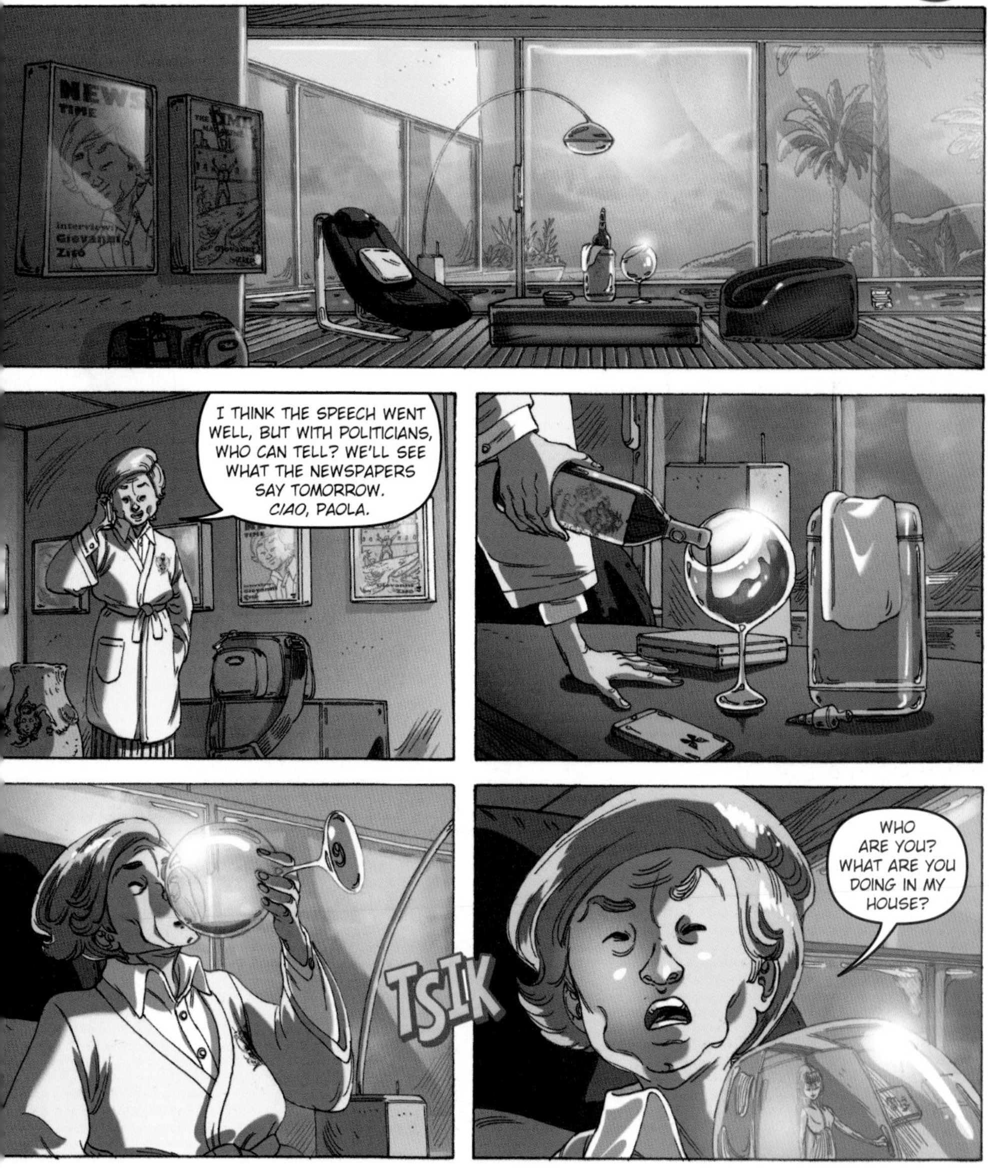

I THINK THE SPEECH WENT WELL, BUT WITH POLITICIANS, WHO CAN TELL? WE'LL SEE WHAT THE NEWSPAPERS SAY TOMORROW. *CIAO*, PAOLA.
TSIK
WHO ARE YOU? WHAT ARE YOU DOING IN MY HOUSE?

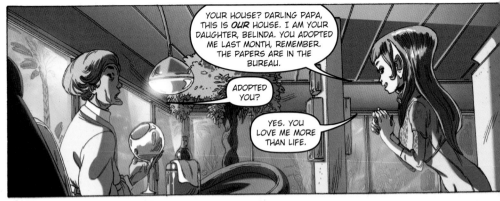

BELOW THE
[TERRANEAN.
V.

I have a sinking feeling deep in the pit of my stomach.

We keep to the older, minor chutes. We fly past stalagmites the size of skyscrapers and over craters teeming with glowing insect life.

But my head is on autopilot.

I'm thinking of Commander Root.

My superior. My friend.

Gone forever.

Only Artemis can help us now.

the past hour, I have literally myself becoming a different mis Fowl as my memories slotted back into place.

ach one changing ho I am.

I'm not exactly as I was before. But close.

I'm hit hard by the loss of Commander Root.

WELL, ARTEMIS, I'VE LANDED THE SHUTTLE. WHAT ARE WE GOING TO DO?

I THINK I SEE HER PLAN. ZITO, WITH OPAL'S HELP, LIQUEFIES HIS ORE HERE, AND IT BEGINS TO SINK DOWN THROUGH THE CRUST.

AT A DEPTH OF ONE HUNDRED AND SIX MILES THE MASS OF MOLTEN ORE COMES WITHIN THREE MILES OF E7—A MAJOR CHUTE THAT RUNS FROM HAVEN CITY AND EMERGES IN SOUTHERN ITALY.

ALL OPAL WOULD HAVE TO DO TO BRING DISASTER TO HAVEN CITY IS BLOW A CRACK BETWEEN THE ORE'S PATH AND CHUTE E7. THEN THE ORE WOULD FOLLOW THE PATH OF LEAST RESISTANCE, AND FLOW INTO THE CHUTE...

...AND DOWN STRAIGHT TO HAVEN CITY.

EXACTLY. MY BEST GUESS IS THAT, EVEN WITH THE BLAST WALLS, HALF THE CITY WOULD BE DESTROYED.

AND THE OTHER HALF WOULD BE LEFT BROADCASTING SIGNALS FOR THE HUMAN WORLD TO HEAR.

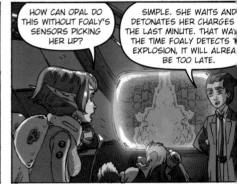

HOW CAN OPAL DO THIS WITHOUT FOALY'S SENSORS PICKING HER UP?

SIMPLE. SHE WAITS AND DETONATES HER CHARGES THE LAST MINUTE. THAT WAY THE TIME FOALY DETECTS THE EXPLOSION, IT WILL ALREA BE TOO LATE.

OKAY, SO ALL WE NEED TO DO IS FIND OPAL'S CHARGES AND REMOVE THEM?

IF ONLY IT WERE THAT SIMPLE. OPAL WILL NOT TAKE ANY CHANCES WITH THINGS GOING WRONG. SHE'LL WAIT UNTIL THE LAST MINUTE TO PLANT HER CHARGES.

SO WE GET INTO THE CHUTE AND WAIT UNTIL SHE PLANTS THE CHARGES?

TOO RISKY. IF FOALY PICK US UP ON HIS SENSORS, TH SEND LEP SHIPS. WE'LL PURSUED AND ARRESTE THANKS TO YOU MURDERI COMMANDER ROOT, REMEMBER?

BUT, ARTEMIS, SURELY EVERYONE MUST KNOW THAT OPAL HAS ESCAPED BY NOW.

THERE'S THE RUB. THAT SINGLE POINT IS THE KEY TO EVERYTHING. PEOPLE OBVIOUSLY *DON'T* KNOW OPAL HAS ESCAPED.

MY BEST GUESS WOULD BE THAT THE OPAL IN CUSTODY IS SOME KIND OF CLONE CRAFTED BY FAIRY TECHNOLOGY. ALIVE, BUT ESSENTIALLY BRAIN-DEAD.

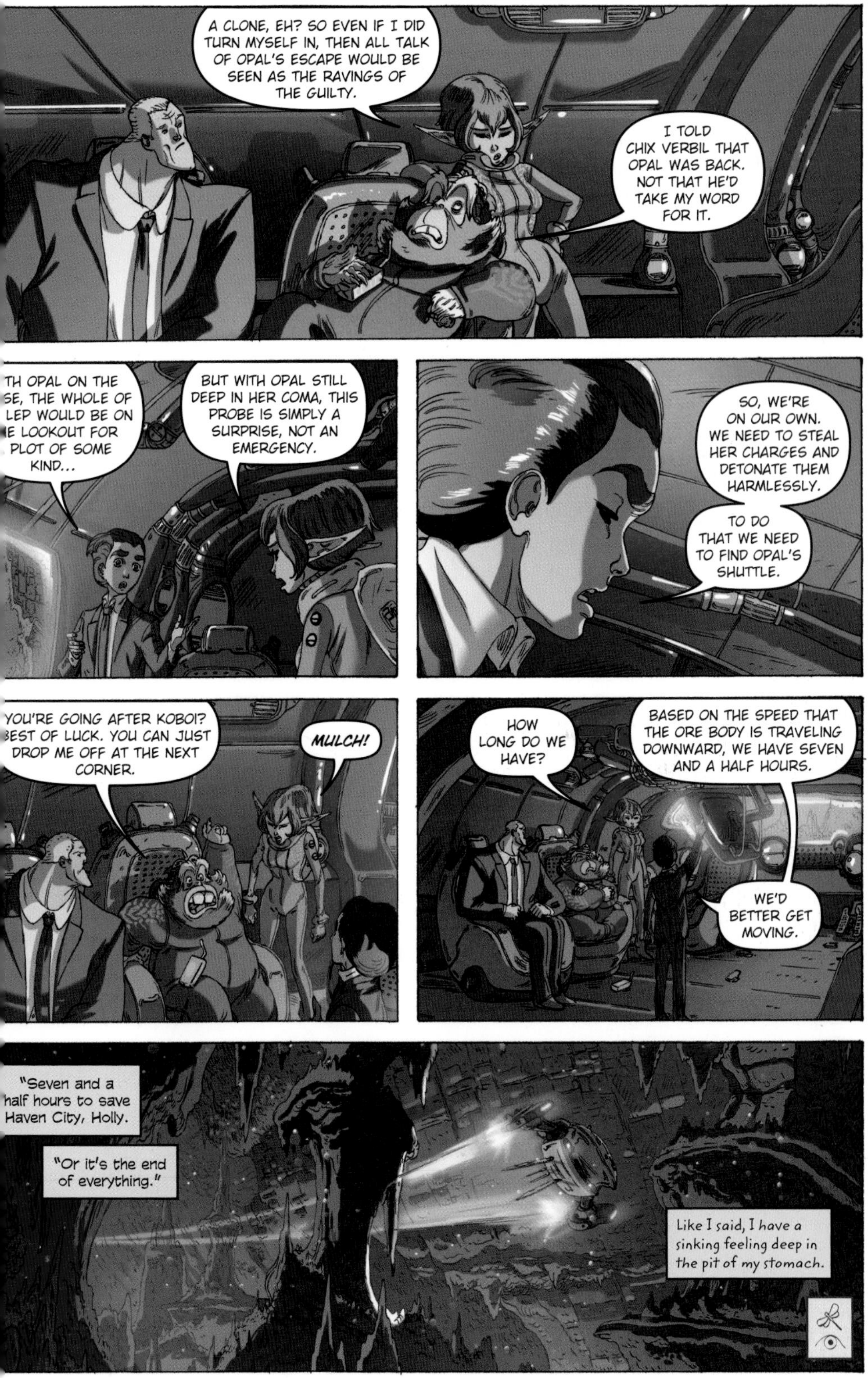
A CLONE, EH? SO EVEN IF I DID TURN MYSELF IN, THEN ALL TALK OF OPAL'S ESCAPE WOULD BE SEEN AS THE RAVINGS OF THE GUILTY.
I TOLD CHIX VERBIL THAT OPAL WAS BACK. NOT THAT HE'D TAKE MY WORD FOR IT.
TH OPAL ON THE SE, THE WHOLE OF LEP WOULD BE ON E LOOKOUT FOR PLOT OF SOME KIND...
BUT WITH OPAL STILL DEEP IN HER COMA, THIS PROBE IS SIMPLY A SURPRISE, NOT AN EMERGENCY.
SO, WE'RE ON OUR OWN. WE NEED TO STEAL HER CHARGES AND DETONATE THEM HARMLESSLY.
TO DO THAT WE NEED TO FIND OPAL'S SHUTTLE.
YOU'RE GOING AFTER KOBOI? BEST OF LUCK. YOU CAN JUST DROP ME OFF AT THE NEXT CORNER.
MULCH!
HOW LONG DO WE HAVE?
BASED ON THE SPEED THAT THE ORE BODY IS TRAVELING DOWNWARD, WE HAVE SEVEN AND A HALF HOURS.
WE'D BETTER GET MOVING.
"Seven and a half hours to save Haven City, Holly.
"Or it's the end of everything."
Like I said, I have a sinking feeling deep in the pit of my stomach.

GIOVANNI ZITO AND THE CORE PROBE

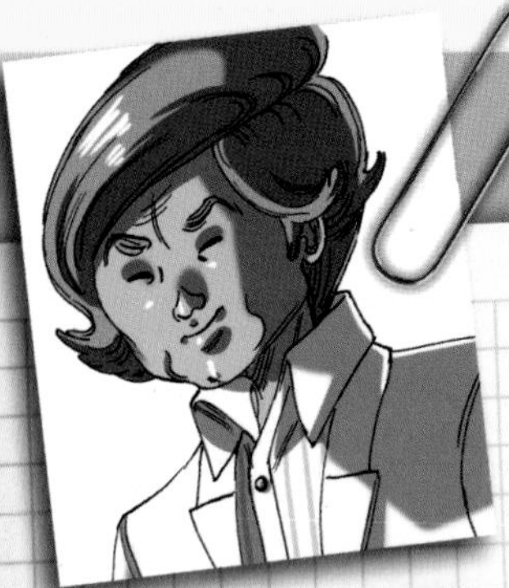

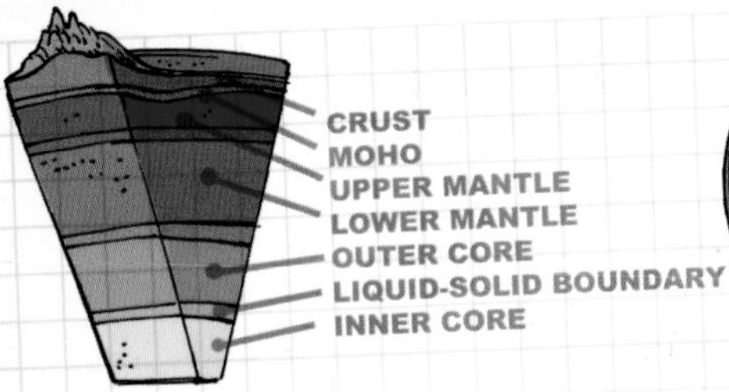
CRUST
MOHO
UPPER MANTLE
LOWER MANTLE
OUTER CORE
LIQUID-SOLID BOUNDARY
INNER CORE

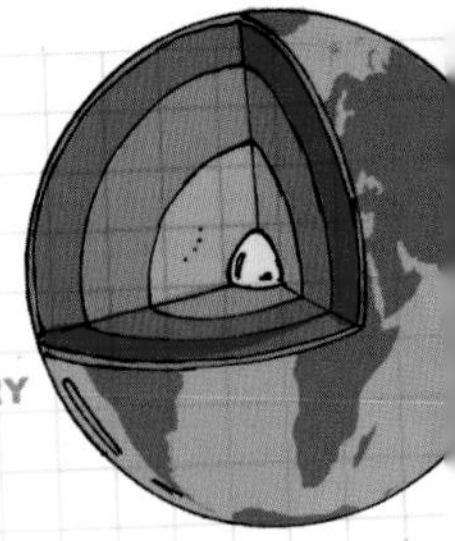

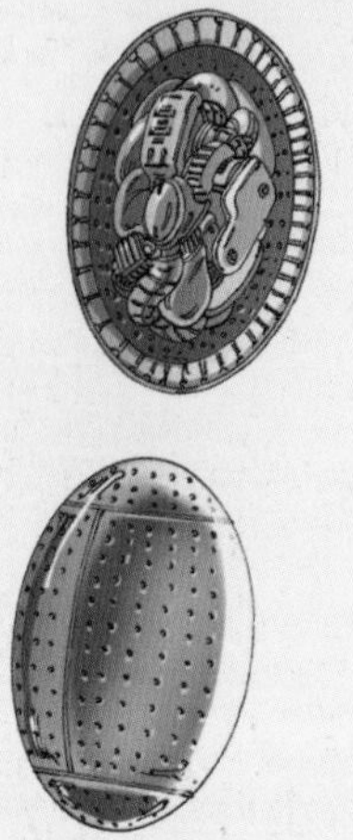

NAME: Giovanni Zito

BACKGROUND: Zito is one of the most famous Italian in the world. This billionaire environmentalist first ca to international fame when he jumped on the back of a humpback whale to save it from whalers' harpoons. Th image became the best selling *TIME* magazine cover of that decade.

ACHIEVEMENTS: Zito has a doctorate in alternative energy. He has spent his life and fortune developing eco-friendly solutions to modern problems, calling his approach "clean sky thinking."

PET PROJECTS IN DEVELOPMENT INCLUDE: The Core Probe Project, a way of exploring earth's inner space, first proposed by planetary scientist professor David Stevenson.

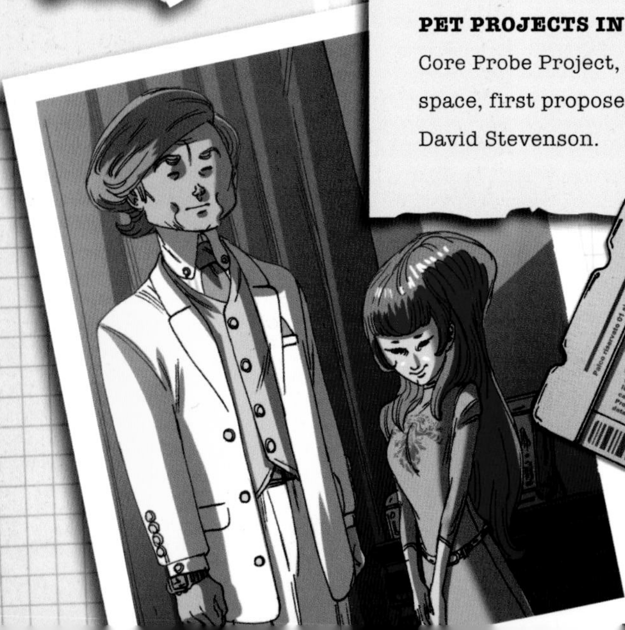

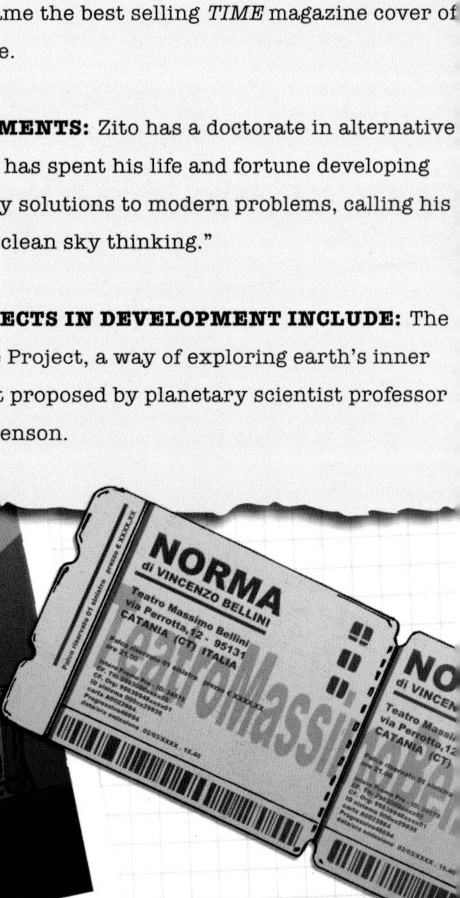
NORMA
di VINCENZO BELLINI
Teatro Massimo Bellini
via Perrotta,12 - 95131
CATANIA (CT) ITALIA
TeatroMassi

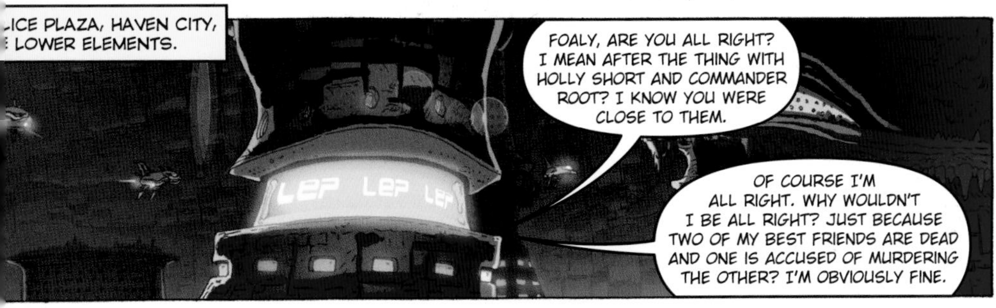
LICE PLAZA, HAVEN CITY,
LOWER ELEMENTS.
FOALY, ARE YOU ALL RIGHT? I MEAN AFTER THE THING WITH HOLLY SHORT AND COMMANDER ROOT? I KNOW YOU WERE CLOSE TO THEM.
OF COURSE I'M ALL RIGHT. WHY WOULDN'T I BE ALL RIGHT? JUST BECAUSE TWO OF MY BEST FRIENDS ARE DEAD AND ONE IS ACCUSED OF MURDERING THE OTHER? I'M OBVIOUSLY FINE.
LEP LEP LEP

HAPTER 10: HORSE SENSE

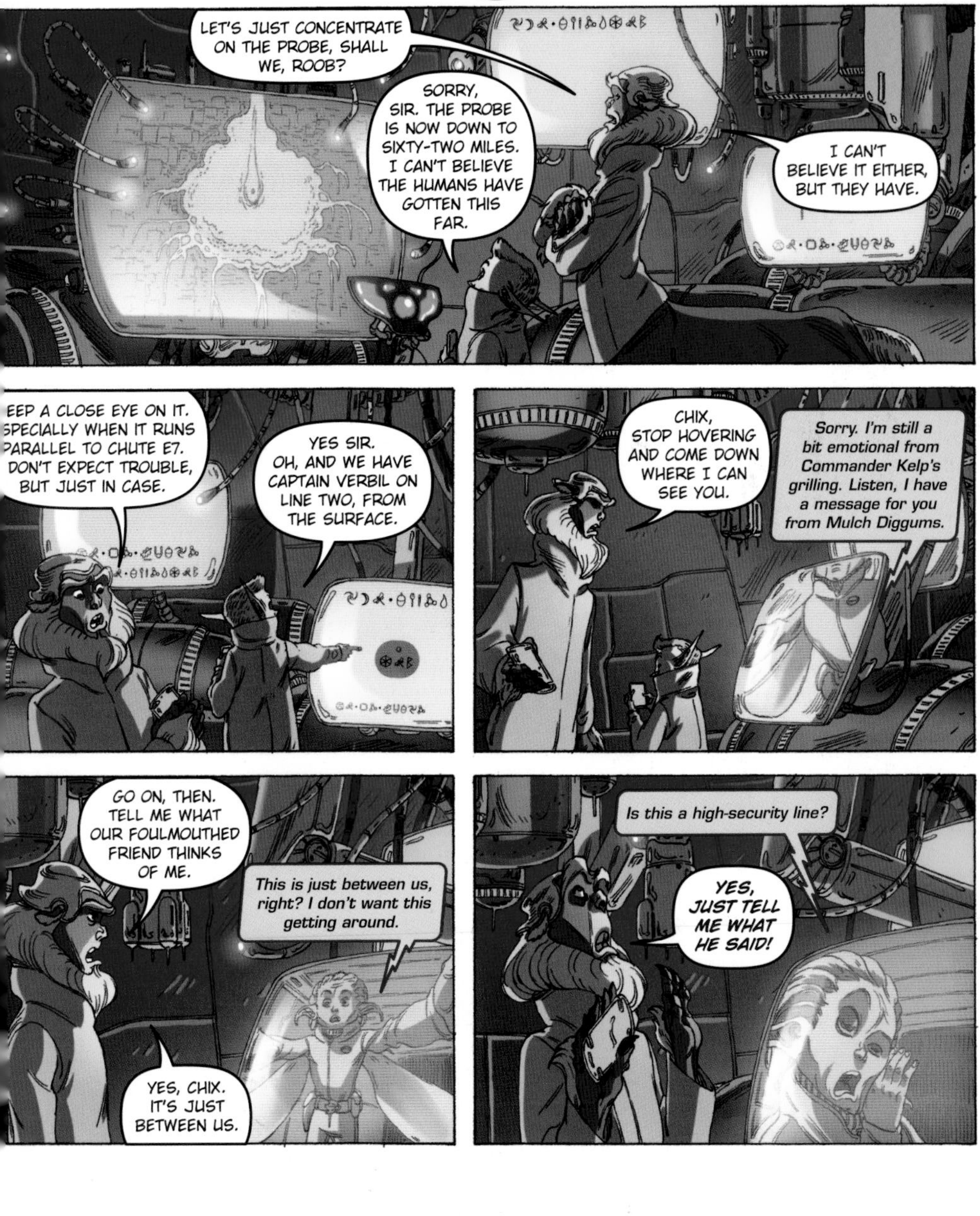
LET'S JUST CONCENTRATE ON THE PROBE, SHALL WE, ROOB?
SORRY, SIR. THE PROBE IS NOW DOWN TO SIXTY-TWO MILES. I CAN'T BELIEVE THE HUMANS HAVE GOTTEN THIS FAR.
I CAN'T BELIEVE IT EITHER, BUT THEY HAVE.
EEP A CLOSE EYE ON IT. SPECIALLY WHEN IT RUNS PARALLEL TO CHUTE E7. DON'T EXPECT TROUBLE, BUT JUST IN CASE.
YES SIR. OH, AND WE HAVE CAPTAIN VERBIL ON LINE TWO, FROM THE SURFACE.
CHIX, STOP HOVERING AND COME DOWN WHERE I CAN SEE YOU.
Sorry. I'm still a bit emotional from Commander Kelp's grilling. Listen, I have a message for you from Mulch Diggums.
GO ON, THEN. TELL ME WHAT OUR FOULMOUTHED FRIEND THINKS OF ME.
This is just between us, right? I don't want this getting around.
YES, CHIX. IT'S JUST BETWEEN US.
Is this a high-security line?
YES, JUST TELL ME WHAT HE SAID!

Opal Koboi is back.

That's what he sa

HA—OPAL ISN'T BACK. DON'T MAKE ME LAUGH. I'M LOOKING AT HER LIVE FEED RIGHT NOW.

SHE'S IN THE ARGON CLINIC, SUSPENDED IN HER COMA HARNESS, AND SHE HAD A DNA SWAB TEST A FEW MINUTES AGO.

I DON'T BLAME YOU FOR BEING TAKEN IN, CHIX. MULCH HAS FOOLED SMARTER SPRITES THAN YOU.

Hey, there's no need for that. I have feelings too you know.

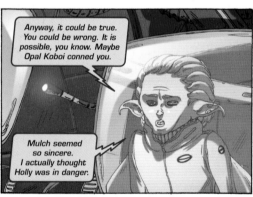

Anyway, it could be true. You could be wrong. It is possible, you know. Maybe Opal Koboi conned you.

Mulch seemed so sincere. I actually thought Holly was in danger.

WHAT? MULCH SAID HOLLY WAS IN DANGER? BUT HOLLY IS GONE. SHE DIED.

I guess Mulch was shoveling more horse dung.

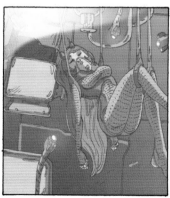

HOLD THE FOR ROOB. I'M GOI TO VISIT AN O FRIEND.

HARTED CHUTE, E MILES BELOW THERN ITALY.

We make good time to the surface. Now for Opal.

TELL ME AGAIN, ARTEMIS. IF WE WANT TO FIND OPAL'S STEALTH SHUTTLE, WHY ARE WE LOOKING FOR EMPTY SPACES?

OUR SENSORS ARE NOWHERE NEAR SOPHISTICATED ENOUGH TO SPOT OPAL'S STEALTH SHUTTLE. BUT I THINK THERE IS A WAY...

AIR IS MADE UP OF VARIOUS S, OF COURSE. GASES LIKE EN, HYDROGEN, AND SO ON. AND HERE'S MY POINT—THE LTH SHUTTLE'S HULL WILL VENT ANY OF THESE FROM BEING DETECTED.

SO IF WE FIND A SMALL PATCH OF SPACE WITHOUT THE USUAL AMBIENT GASES, THEN...

...THEN THAT HOLE IN THE AIR IS THE STEALTH SHUTTLE.

EXACTLY.

IF WE ASSUME THAT THE STEALTH SHUTTLE IS GOING TO BE VERY CLOSE TO CHUTE E7, THAT'S STILL A LOT OF GROUND TO SCAN, BUT LET'S TRY.

Three gas anomalies located.

THAT'S PROBABLY AN AIRPORT. LOTS OF EXHAUST FUMES.

THAT VACUUM IS PROBABLY A COMPUTER PLANT ON THE SURFACE.

AH, THERE...

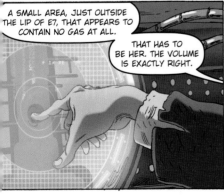

A SMALL AREA, JUST OUTSIDE THE LIP OF E7, THAT APPEARS TO CONTAIN NO GAS AT ALL.

THAT HAS TO BE HER. THE VOLUME IS EXACTLY RIGHT.

YOU REALIZE THAT AS SOON AS WE MOVE INTO THE MAIN CHUTE, FOALY WILL SPOT US AND WE'LL BE OUTLAWS?

LET'S HOPE WE CAN SAVE HAVEN CITY SO WE CAN KEEP BEING OUTLAWS. AT LEAST FOR NOW.

THE ARGON CLINIC, HAVEN CITY.

THIS IS OUTRAGEOUS. WHO KNOWS WHAT EFFECT YOUR DEVICES MIGHT HAVE ON HER RECOVERING PSYCHE? I UTTERLY FORBID IT.

I DO HOPE YOU'RE NOT THINKING OF OPAL AS YOUR PERSONAL POSSESSION, DR. ARGON. SHE IS A STATE PRISONER, AND I CAN HAVE HER MOVED OUT OF HERE ANY TIME I LIKE.

MAYB FIVE MIN WOULD HURT

WHAT HAVE YOU GOT THERE, ANYWAY?

DON'T WORRY. IT'S JUST A RETIMAGER.

EVERY IMAGE IS RECORDED ON RETINAS. THIS LEA A TRAIL OF MICROSC SCRATCHES THA CAN BE ENHANCED READ. MY OWN INVENTION.

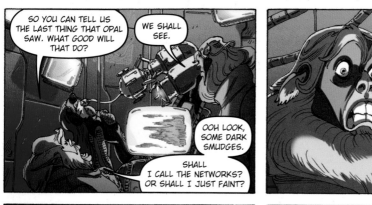

SO YOU CAN TELL US THE LAST THING THAT OPAL SAW. WHAT GOOD WILL THAT DO?

WE SHALL SEE.

OOH LOOK, SOME DARK SMUDGES.

SHALL I CALL THE NETWORKS? OR SHALL I JUST FAINT?

COMPUTER, LIGHTEN IMAGE AND ENHANCE AND WE SHOULD SEE...

SHE SAW HERSELF FROM THE SIDE. THAT MEANS THERE WERE TWO OPAL KOBOIS. TWO. THE REAL ONE THAT YOU LET ESCAPE AND THIS SHELL HERE.

OH, DEAR.

"OH, DEAR" HARDLY COVERS IT.

MAYBE NOW WOU BE A GOOD TO CALL NETWORK OR FAINT AWE.

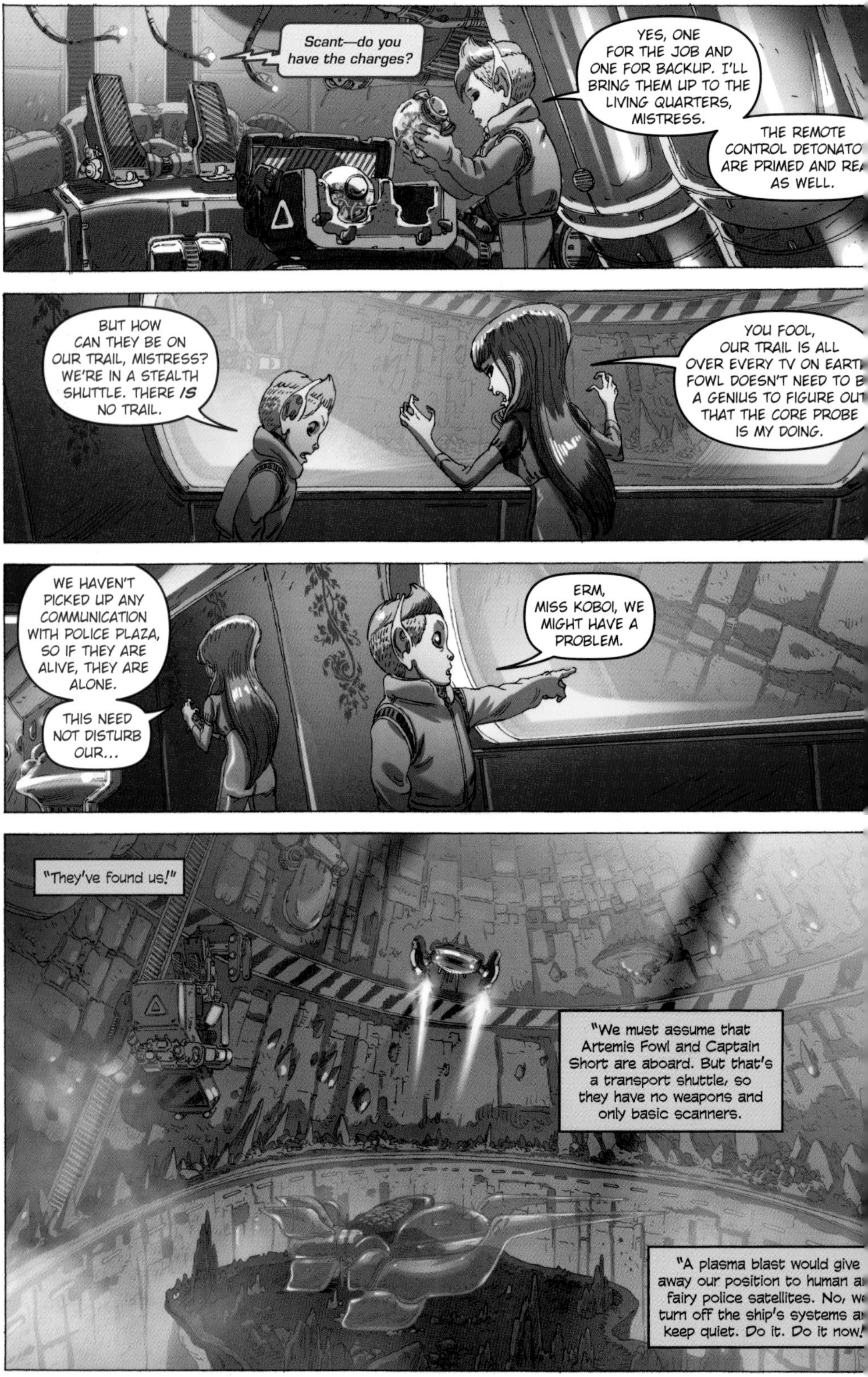
Scant—do you have the charges?
YES, ONE FOR THE JOB AND ONE FOR BACKUP. I'LL BRING THEM UP TO THE LIVING QUARTERS, MISTRESS.
THE REMOTE CONTROL DETONATO ARE PRIMED AND RE AS WELL.
BUT HOW CAN THEY BE ON OUR TRAIL, MISTRESS? WE'RE IN A STEALTH SHUTTLE. THERE *IS* NO TRAIL.
YOU FOOL, OUR TRAIL IS ALL OVER EVERY TV ON EART FOWL DOESN'T NEED TO B A GENIUS TO FIGURE OUT THAT THE CORE PROBE IS MY DOING.
WE HAVEN'T PICKED UP ANY COMMUNICATION WITH POLICE PLAZA, SO IF THEY ARE ALIVE, THEY ARE ALONE.
THIS NEED NOT DISTURB OUR…
ERM, MISS KOBOI, WE MIGHT HAVE A PROBLEM.
"They've found us!"
"We must assume that Artemis Fowl and Captain Short are aboard. But that's a transport shuttle, so they have no weapons and only basic scanners.
"A plasma blast would give away our position to human a fairy police satellites. No, w turn off the ship's systems a keep quiet. Do it. Do it now!

CRRRUNCH

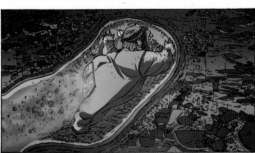

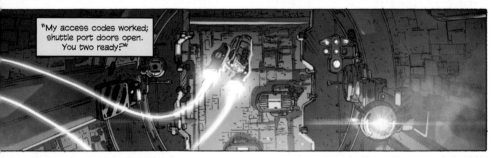

"My access codes worked; shuttle port doors open. You two ready?"

WE'RE READY, HOLLY. FLY IN A GRID SEARCH PATTERN AS THOUGH WE'RE NOT CERTAIN WHERE THE STEALTH SHUTTLE IS.

NOW, OLD FRIEND, CAN YOU MAKE CERTAIN THAT OPAL IS LOOKING THIS WAY?

BOOOOMMMMM!!

"I bet that got her attention."

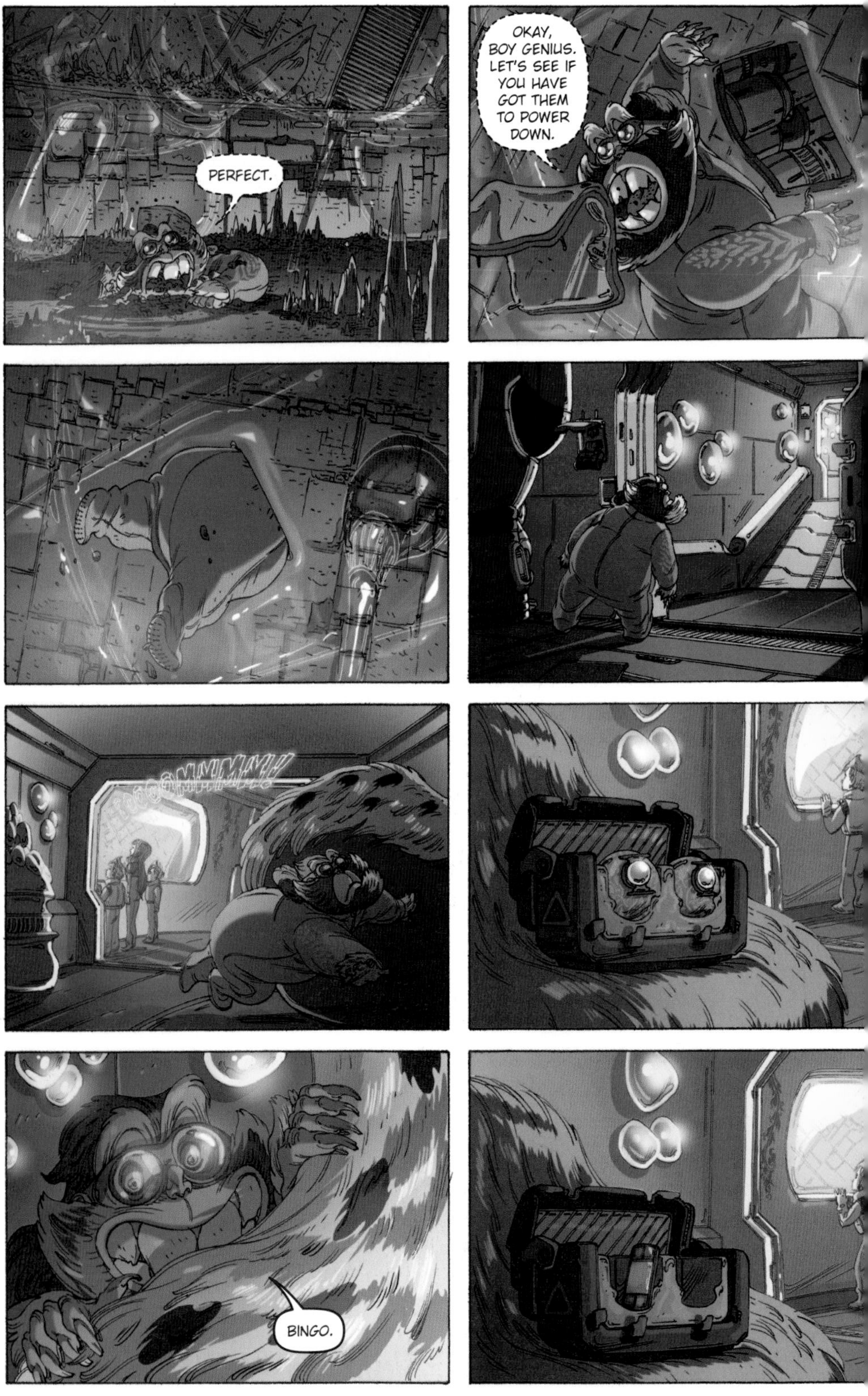
PERFECT.
OKAY, BOY GENIUS. LET'S SEE IF YOU HAVE GOT THEM TO POWER DOWN.
BINGO.

OWL MUST HAVE GUESSED HERE WE ARE BECAUSE OF E CHUTE'S PROXIMITY TO THE ROBE. BUT ALL HE HAS IS AN APPROXIMATION.

ALL WE NEED O DO IT STAY QUIET ND CALM. EVEN IF A RENADE HITS US, IT WON'T PENETRATE THE HULL.

IT WOULD BE A DELIGHT TO BLOW THEM OUT OF THE SKY. BUT THAT WOULD ONLY LIGHT UP FOALY'S SATELLITE SCANNERS AND PAINT A BULL'S-EYE ON OUR HULL.

'RE HEADING AWAY, 'TRESS. BACK DOWN THE CHUTE.

HMM...SURPRISING. WHY WOULD THEY DO THAT?

AT LEAST WE'RE OKAY, MISTRESS.

YOU IMBECILE. WE WERE ALWAYS GOING TO BE OKAY.

THOSE EXPLOSIVES COULDN'T HAVE HURT US BECAUSE...

EMIS WOULD KNOW T THOSE GRENADES LDN'T HURT US, SO HY DROP THEM? UNLESS...

THEY WERE JUST A DISTRACTION... OH, NO!

THE CHARGES? WHERE ARE THEY?

WHILE WE WERE WATCHING THE PRETTY LIGHTS OUTSIDE LIKE FOOLS, SOMEONE HAS BEEN IN HERE.

THEY'VE TAKEN THE CHARGES. AND LEFT US THIS... COMMUNICATOR.

SOMETHING TO TAUNT ME WITH LATER, NO DOUBT.

FOLLOW THAT SHUTTLE.

AT THE VERY LEAST, WE CAN STILL DETONATE THE CHARGES AND DESTROY MY ENEMIES.

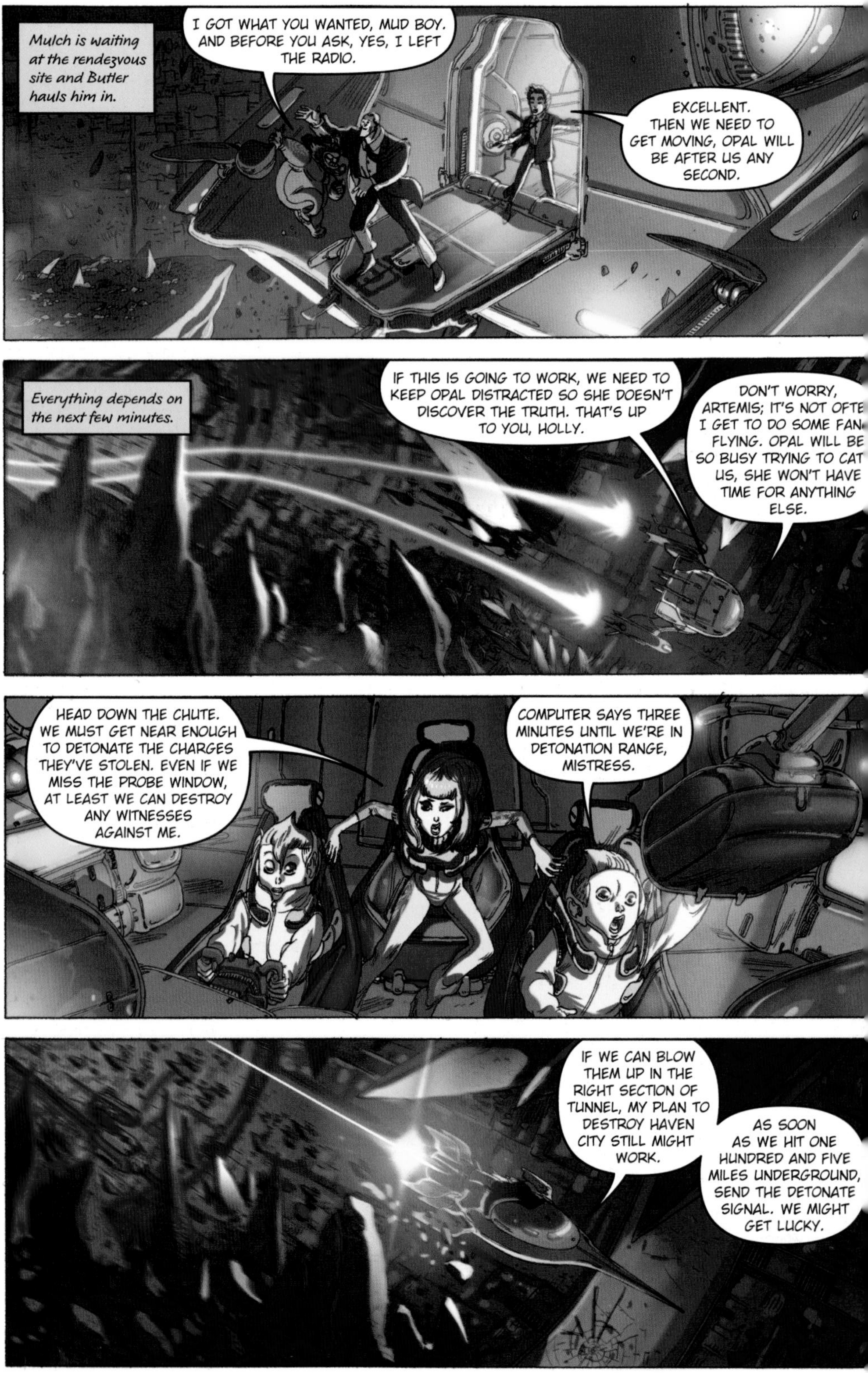
Mulch is waiting at the rendezvous site and Butler hauls him in.
I GOT WHAT YOU WANTED, MUD BOY. AND BEFORE YOU ASK, YES, I LEFT THE RADIO.
EXCELLENT. THEN WE NEED TO GET MOVING, OPAL WILL BE AFTER US ANY SECOND.
Everything depends on the next few minutes.
IF THIS IS GOING TO WORK, WE NEED TO KEEP OPAL DISTRACTED SO SHE DOESN'T DISCOVER THE TRUTH. THAT'S UP TO YOU, HOLLY.
DON'T WORRY, ARTEMIS; IT'S NOT OFTE I GET TO DO SOME FAN FLYING. OPAL WILL BE SO BUSY TRYING TO CAT US, SHE WON'T HAVE TIME FOR ANYTHING ELSE.
HEAD DOWN THE CHUTE. WE MUST GET NEAR ENOUGH TO DETONATE THE CHARGES THEY'VE STOLEN. EVEN IF WE MISS THE PROBE WINDOW, AT LEAST WE CAN DESTROY ANY WITNESSES AGAINST ME.
COMPUTER SAYS THREE MINUTES UNTIL WE'RE IN DETONATION RANGE, MISTRESS.
IF WE CAN BLOW THEM UP IN THE RIGHT SECTION OF TUNNEL, MY PLAN TO DESTROY HAVEN CITY STILL MIGHT WORK.
AS SOON AS WE HIT ONE HUNDRED AND FIVE MILES UNDERGROUND, SEND THE DETONATE SIGNAL. WE MIGHT GET LUCKY.

insides feel like they're trying
...rce their way out through my
...at. I'm not the only one.

IS ALL THIS JIGGLING ABOUT REALLY NECESSARY? I'VE HAD A LOT TO EAT RECENTLY, EVEN FOR A DWARF.

WE'RE AT A DEPTH OF ONE ZERO FIVE NOW. OPAL WILL BE TRYING TO DETONATE. SHE'S CLOSING FAST.

WE'RE NEARLY THERE, MULCH. TELL BUTLER TO OPEN THE BAG.

Y...ARE YOU ...E OPAL WILL ...WHAT SHE'S ...UPPOSED TO?

OF COURSE I AM. IT'S HUMAN NATURE AND OPAL IS A HUMAN NOW, REMEMBER? OKAY, HOLLY. PULL OVER.

...U'RE NOT GOING ...BELIEVE THIS, OP— ...MISS KOBOI.

DON'T TELL ME THEY'VE STOPPED?

YES, THEY ARE HOVERING AT A HUNDRED AND TWENTY-FOUR MILES. WHY WOULD THEY DO THAT?

JUST KEEP SENDING THE DETONATION SIGNAL SO WE CAN...

BEEP BEEP BEEP

AH, HERE WE GO. THEY'RE GETTING IN TOUCH.

Opal, I am giving you one chance to surrender. We have disarmed your charges and the LEP are on their way. Turn yourself over to Captain Short.

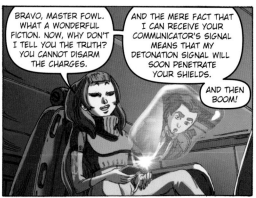

BRAVO, MASTER FOWL. WHAT A WONDERFUL FICTION. NOW, WHY DON'T I TELL YOU THE TRUTH? YOU CANNOT DISARM THE CHARGES.

AND THE MERE FACT THAT I CAN RECEIVE YOUR COMMUNICATOR'S SIGNAL MEANS THAT MY DETONATION SIGNAL WILL SOON PENETRATE YOUR SHIELDS.

AND THEN BOOM!

YOU CANNOT JETTIS THE CHARGES OR I' DETONATE THEM IN T CHUTE. AND THERE IS LEP ON THE WAY T HELP YOU.

YOU ARE OBVIOUSLY ATTEMPTING TO STALL ME UNTIL THE OREBOD AND PROBE PASSES YOUR DEPTH.

So you refuse to surrender?

YOU ARE ABOUT TO DIE, ARTEMIS FOWL.

SO YES, I THINK I WILL FIGHT ON.

Well, if we do die, at least it'll be on full stomachs. Mulch took something else from your shuttle. Something rather delicious.

MY TRUFFLES? YOU STOLE MY TRUFFLES? THAT'S JUST **MEAN**.

They really do melt in the mouth.

KILLING YOU ALL IS GOING TO BE **SUCH** A PLEASURE.

MERV, DO WE HAVE A DETONATION SIGNAL YET?

Keep trying, Merv. —click—

THAT'S IT, SHE'S GONE. IS THIS GOING TO WORK, ARTEMIS?

FROM THE LOOK ON HER FACE, I'D BET MY LIFE ON IT.

GOOD, BECAUSE I THINK YOU JUST DID.

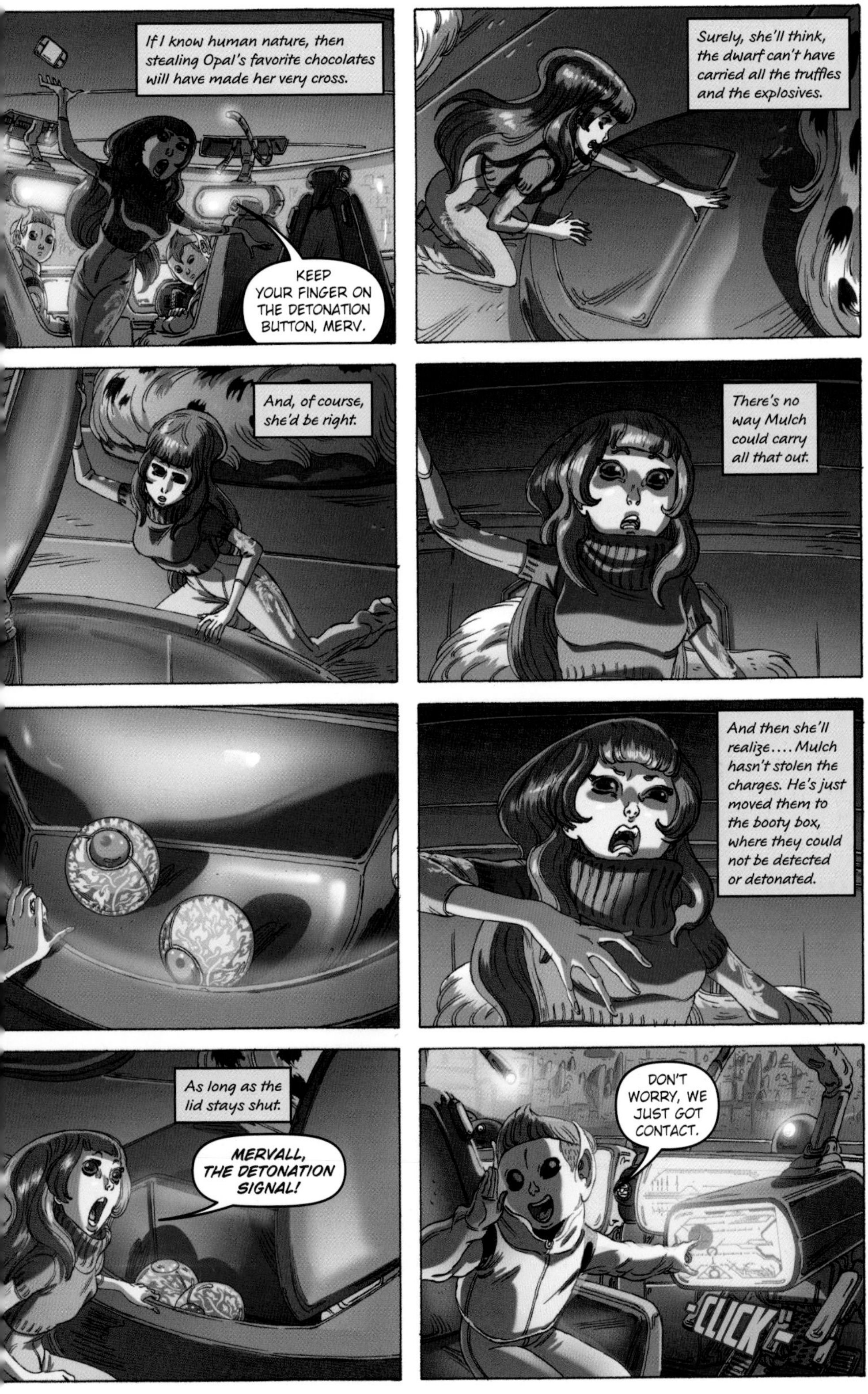
If I know human nature, then stealing Opal's favorite chocolates will have made her very cross.
KEEP YOUR FINGER ON THE DETONATION BUTTON, MERV.
Surely, she'll think, the dwarf can't have carried all the truffles and the explosives.
And, of course, she'd be right.
There's no way Mulch could carry all that out.
And then she'll realize.... Mulch hasn't stolen the charges. He's just moved them to the booty box, where they could not be detected or detonated.
As long as the lid stays shut.
MERVALL, THE DETONATION SIGNAL!
DON'T WORRY, WE JUST GOT CONTACT.
CLICK

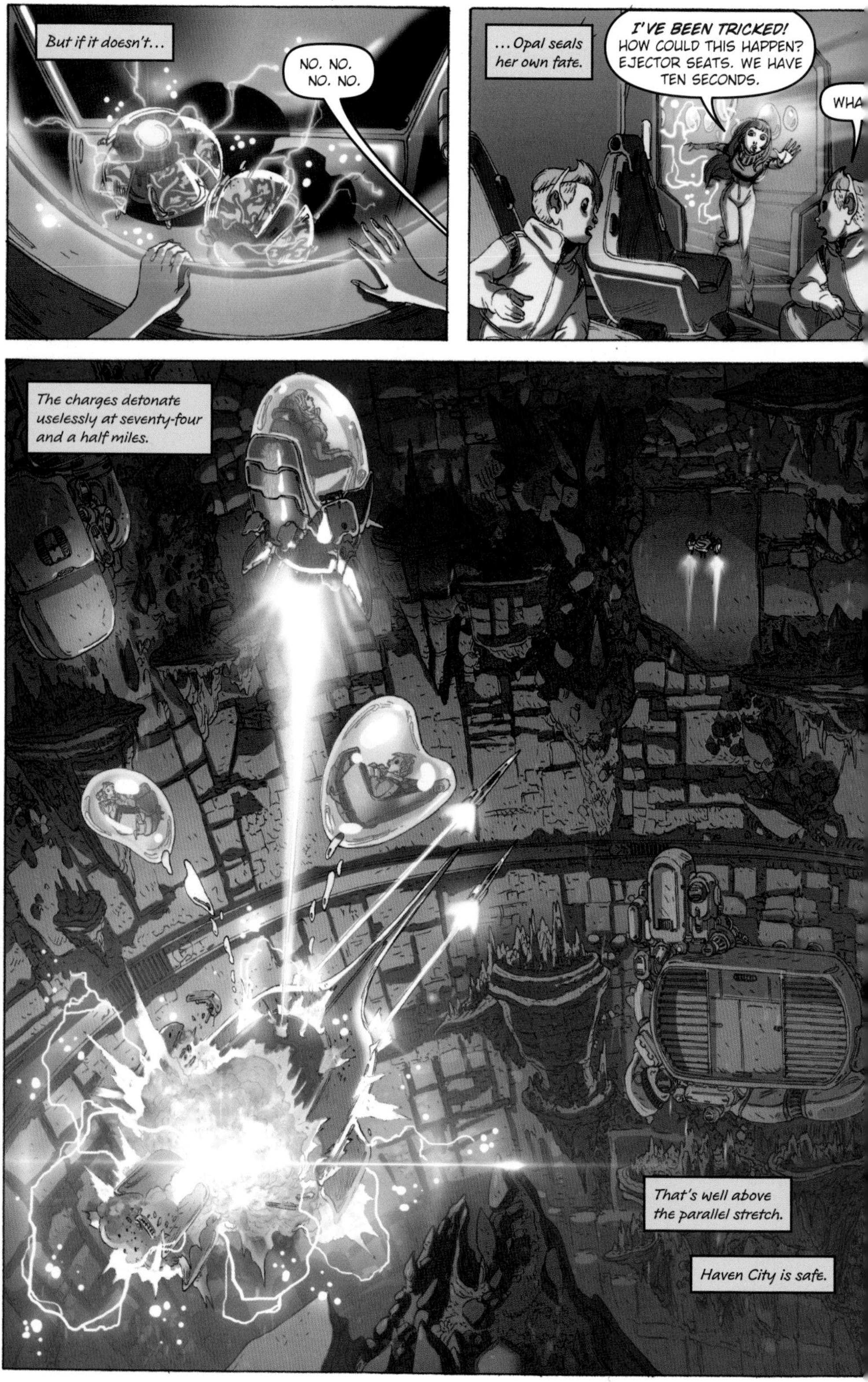
But if it doesn't...
NO. NO.
NO. NO.
...Opal seals her own fate.
I'VE BEEN TRICKED! HOW COULD THIS HAPPEN? EJECTOR SEATS. WE HAVE TEN SECONDS.
WHA
The charges detonate uselessly at seventy-four and a half miles.
That's well above the parallel stretch.
Haven City is safe.

...y pulls our shuttle close ...e chute wall to avoid the ...ng debris, but it's not over.

THOSE TWO DOTS ARE ESCAPE PODS, BUT...OH NO.

THE OTHER TWO AREN'T. OPAL HAS LAUNCHED TWO HEAT-SEEKING MISSILES AND THEY'RE HEADING STRAIGHT FOR US.

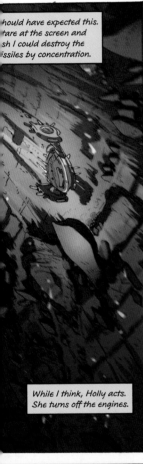

...hould have expected this. ...tare at the screen and ...sh I could destroy the ...issiles by concentration.

While I think, Holly acts. She turns off the engines.

We fall like a stone.

The rushing air cools the engines and our heat signature drops.

Butler uses foam from the fire extinguishers to help cool the engines.

Two seconds to impact...

And I see the missiles veer away from us.

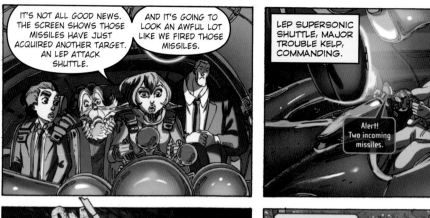

CHAPTER 11: THE LAST GOOD-BYE

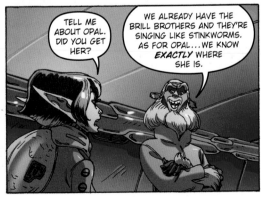

"We think we know what happened...

"Opal's escape capsul[e] limped to the surface, leaking plasma as it wer[e]

"She made it almost te[n] miles across country bef[ore] she ditched in a vineyar[d]

THESE VINES ARE ALL I HAVE.

I'M ALONE. WHO ARE YOU TO CRASH YOUR LITTLE AIRPLANE AND DESTROY THEM?

YOU HAVE ME NOW. I AM YOUR DAUGHTER, BELINDA.

I HAVE A DAUGHTER[.] WELL, THEN GET A SH[OVEL] AND CLEAN UP THIS M[ESS] OR YOU'LL GO TO BE[D] HUNGRY.

"Judging from the satellite images, we think that was the moment her fairy magic ran out."

I DON'T DO PHYSICAL WORK. YOU WILL SERVE ME.

THAT IS NOW YOUR PURPOSE IN LIFE.

DON'T SPEAK SUCH POISON. NOW PICK UP YOUR SHOVEL AND WORK. *WORK!*

"By the time the LEP retriev[al] team get there, I bet she'll b[e] almost happy to see them."

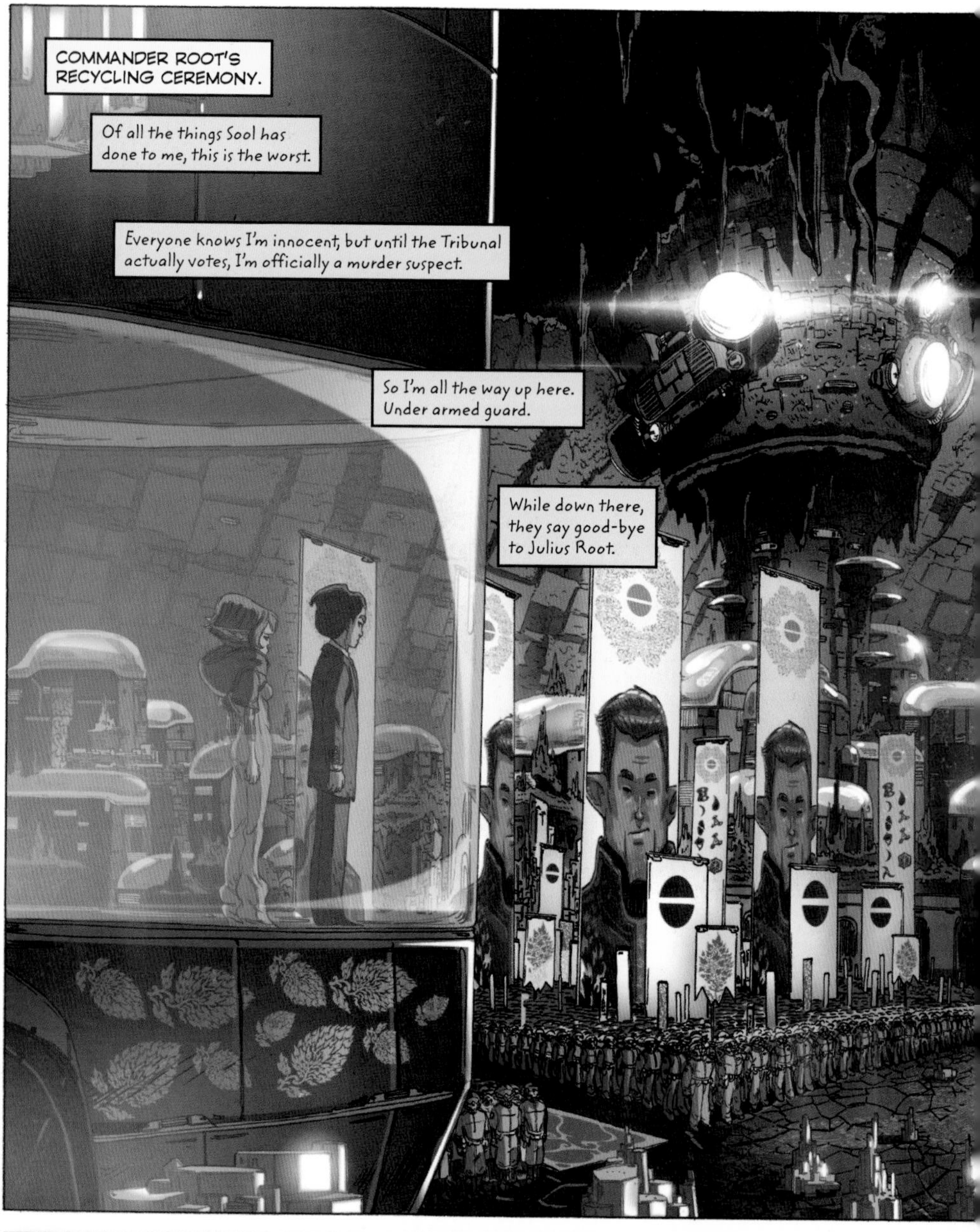

COMMANDER ROOT'S RECYCLING CEREMONY.
Of all the things Sool has done to me, this is the worst.
Everyone knows I'm innocent, but until the Tribunal actually votes, I'm officially a murder suspect.
So I'm all the way up here. Under armed guard.
While down there, they say good-bye to Julius Root.

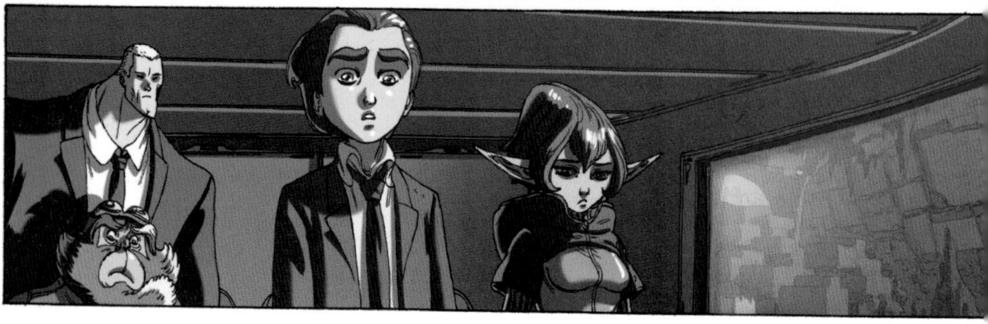

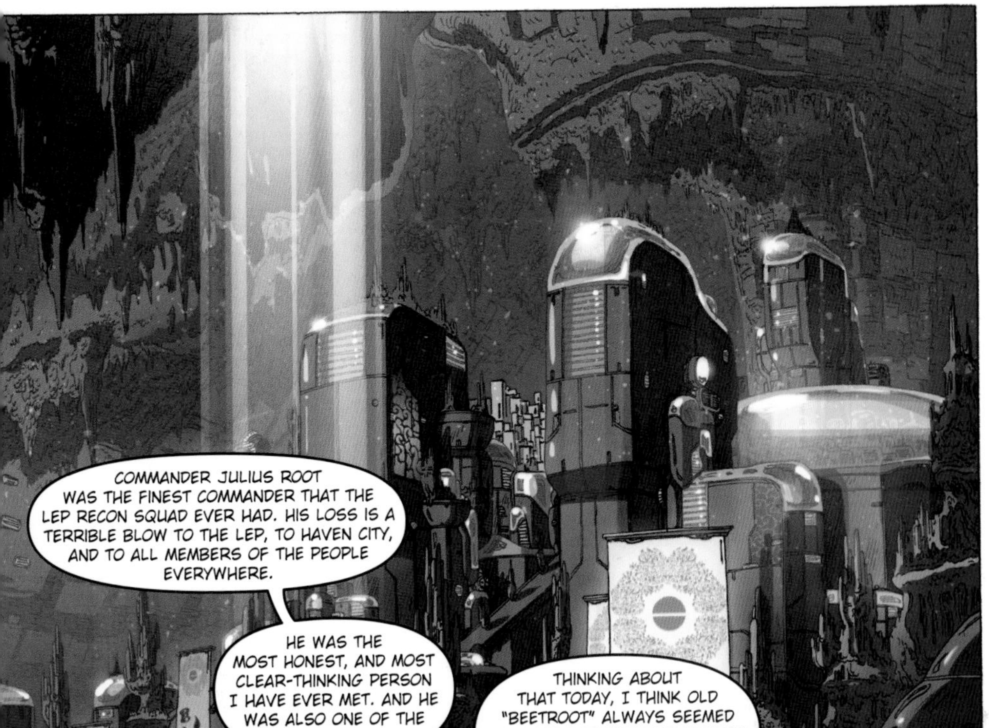
COMMANDER JULIUS ROOT WAS THE FINEST COMMANDER THAT THE LEP RECON SQUAD EVER HAD. HIS LOSS IS A TERRIBLE BLOW TO THE LEP, TO HAVEN CITY, AND TO ALL MEMBERS OF THE PEOPLE EVERYWHERE.
HE WAS THE MOST HONEST, AND MOST CLEAR-THINKING PERSON I HAVE EVER MET. AND HE WAS ALSO ONE OF THE ANGRIEST.
THINKING ABOUT THAT TODAY, I THINK OLD "BEETROOT" ALWAYS SEEMED SO ANGRY BECAUSE HE WANTED EVERYONE TO BE THE BEST THAT THEY POSSIBLY COULD BE. LIKE HIM.
Foaly has even rigged the city's artificial lights to create a holographic sunset.
It's a nice touch, and it makes me cry. Even more.

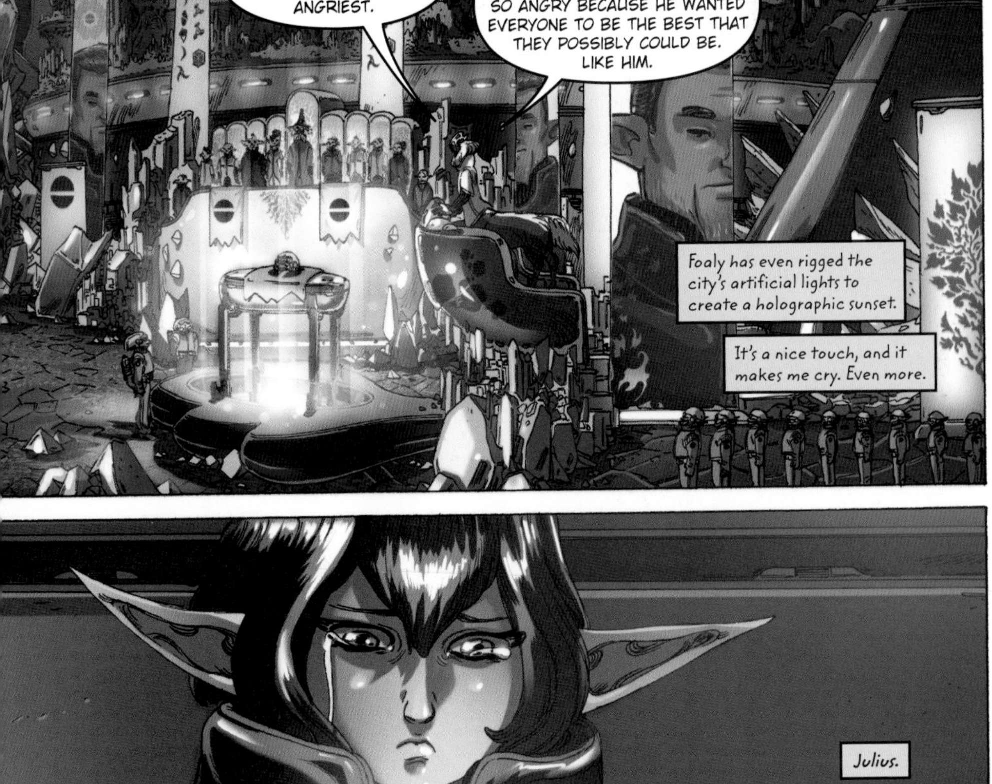
Julius.

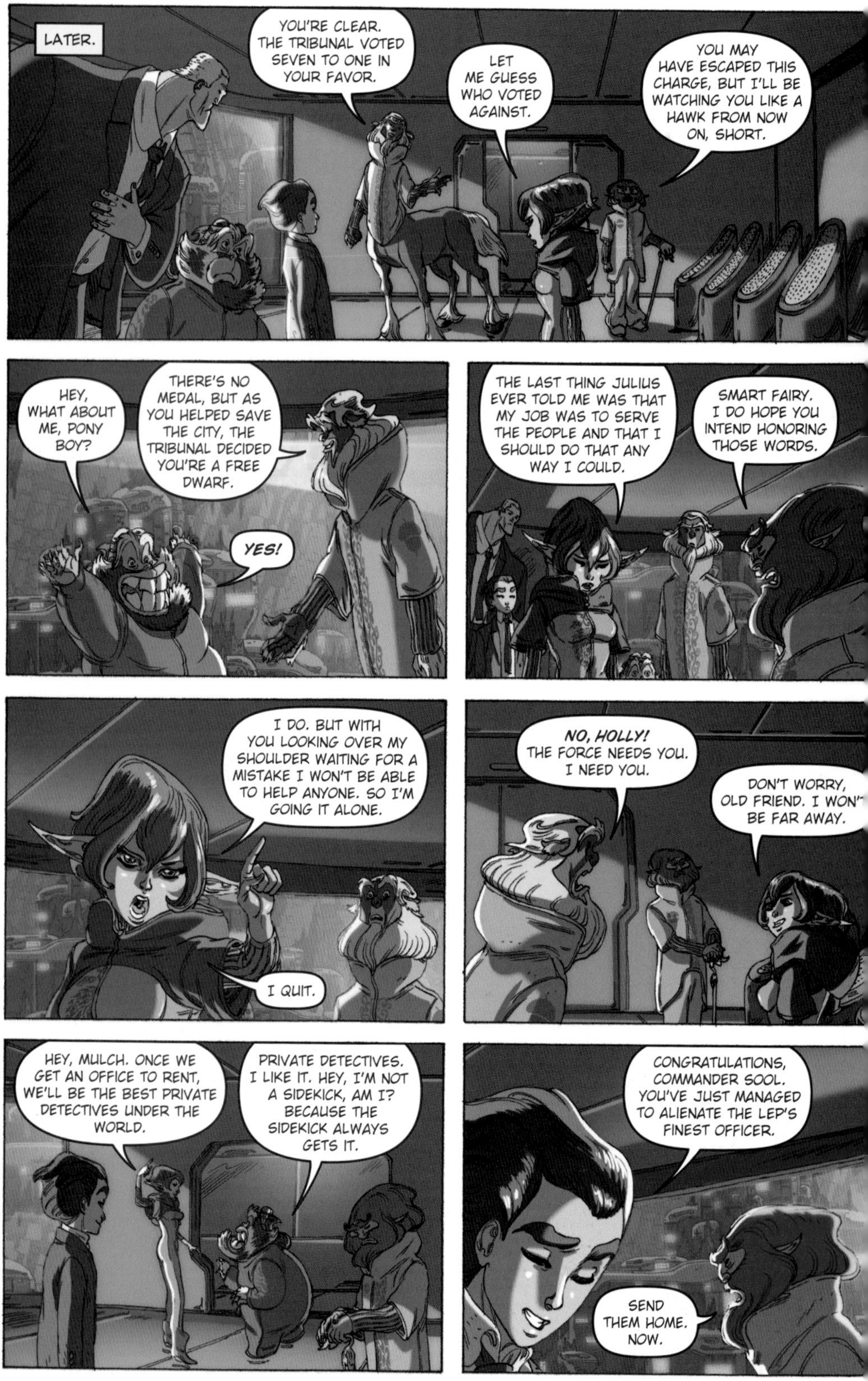
LATER.
YOU'RE CLEAR. THE TRIBUNAL VOTED SEVEN TO ONE IN YOUR FAVOR.
LET ME GUESS WHO VOTED AGAINST.
YOU MAY HAVE ESCAPED THIS CHARGE, BUT I'LL BE WATCHING YOU LIKE A HAWK FROM NOW ON, SHORT.
HEY, WHAT ABOUT ME, PONY BOY?
THERE'S NO MEDAL, BUT AS YOU HELPED SAVE THE CITY, THE TRIBUNAL DECIDED YOU'RE A FREE DWARF.
YES!
THE LAST THING JULIUS EVER TOLD ME WAS THAT MY JOB WAS TO SERVE THE PEOPLE AND THAT I SHOULD DO THAT ANY WAY I COULD.
SMART FAIRY. I DO HOPE YOU INTEND HONORING THOSE WORDS.
I DO. BUT WITH YOU LOOKING OVER MY SHOULDER WAITING FOR A MISTAKE I WON'T BE ABLE TO HELP ANYONE. SO I'M GOING IT ALONE.
I QUIT.
NO, HOLLY! THE FORCE NEEDS YOU. I NEED YOU.
DON'T WORRY, OLD FRIEND. I WON'T BE FAR AWAY.
HEY, MULCH. ONCE WE GET AN OFFICE TO RENT, WE'LL BE THE BEST PRIVATE DETECTIVES UNDER THE WORLD.
PRIVATE DETECTIVES. I LIKE IT. HEY, I'M NOT A SIDEKICK, AM I? BECAUSE THE SIDEKICK ALWAYS GETS IT.
CONGRATULATIONS, COMMANDER SOOL. YOU'VE JUST MANAGED TO ALIENATE THE LEP'S FINEST OFFICER.
SEND THEM HOME. NOW.

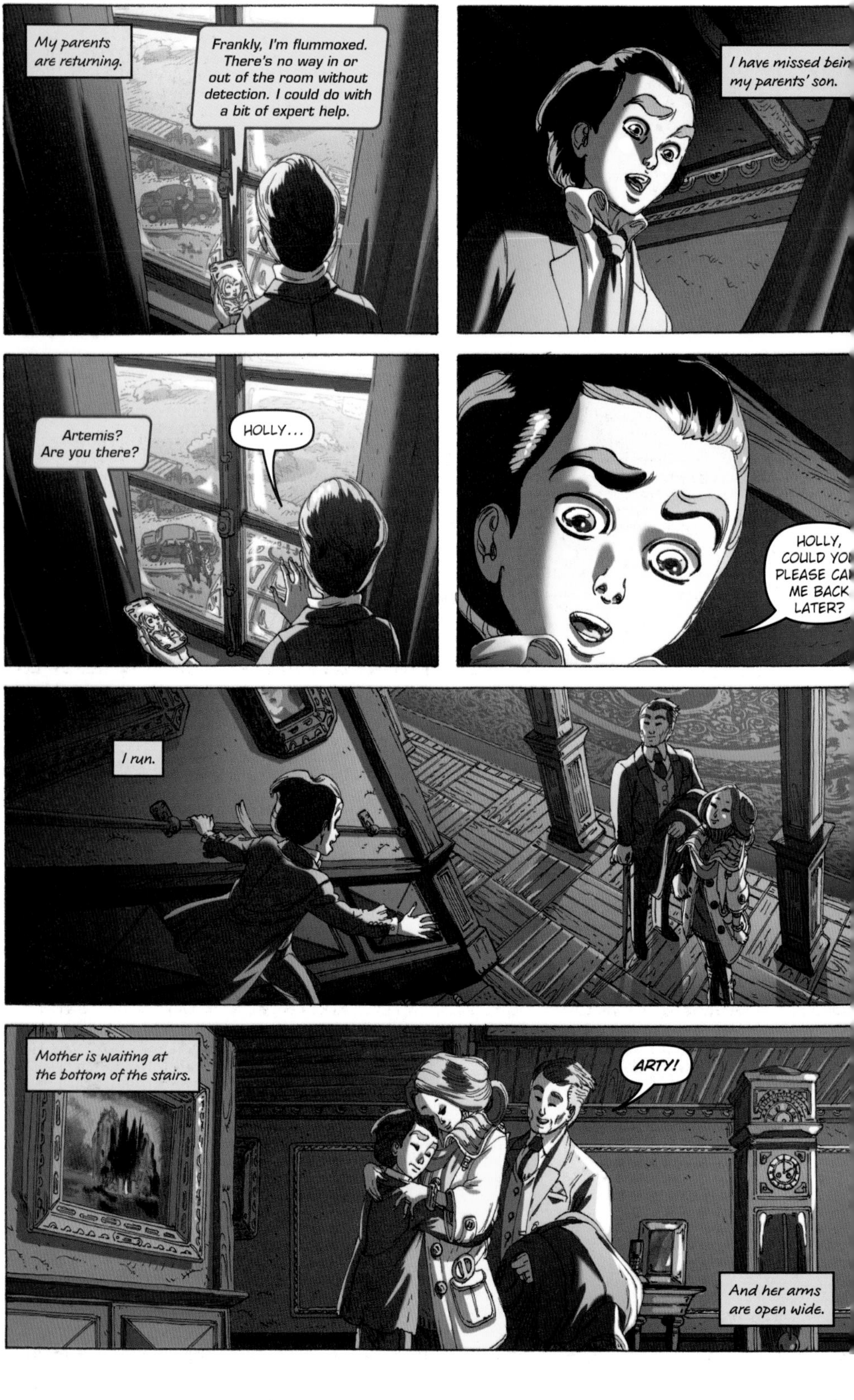

My parents are returning.
Frankly, I'm flummoxed. There's no way in or out of the room without detection. I could do with a bit of expert help.
I have missed bein
my parents' son.
Artemis? Are you there?
HOLLY...
HOLLY, COULD YO PLEASE CA ME BACK LATER?
I run.
Mother is waiting at the bottom of the stairs.
ARTY!
And her arms are open wide.

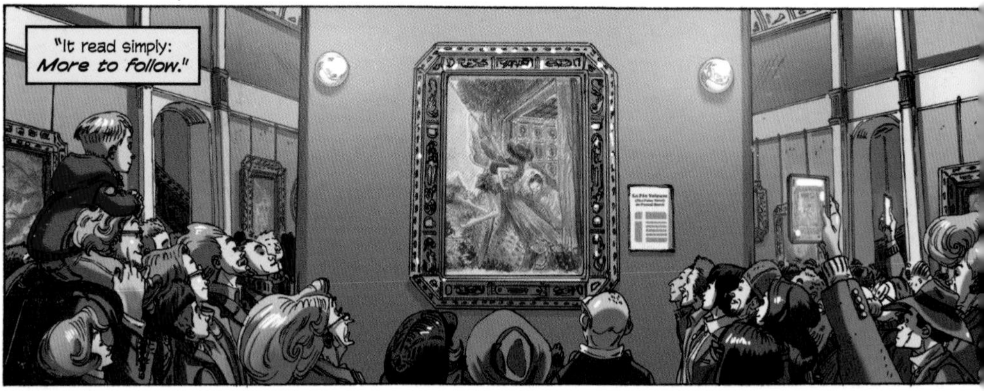
"It read simply: *More to follow.*"

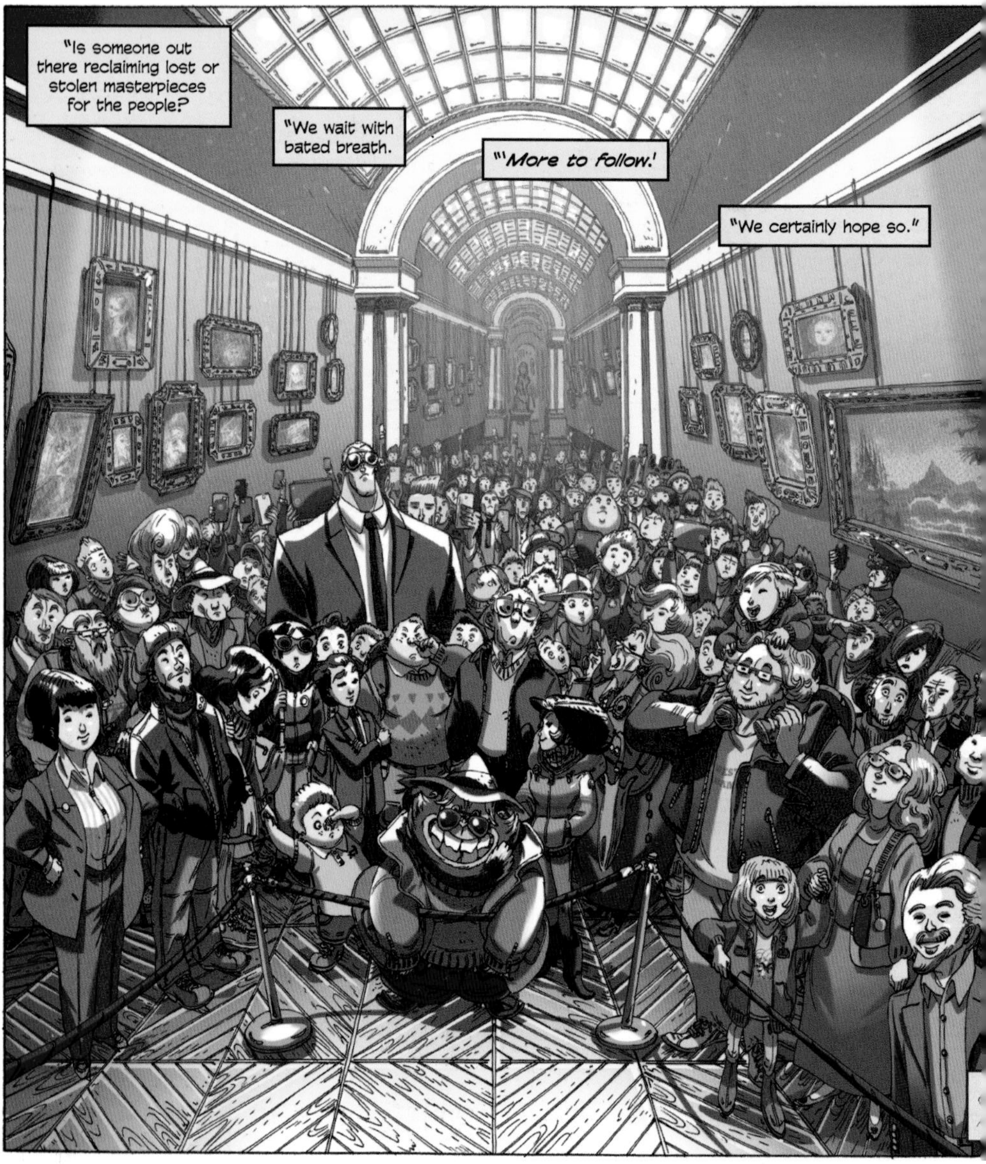
"Is someone out there reclaiming lost or stolen masterpieces for the people?
"We wait with bated breath.
"'*More to follow.*'
"We certainly hope so."